The Good Neighbor

ALSO BY AMY SUE NATHAN

The Glass Wives

The Good Neighbor

A NOVEL

Amy Sue Nathan

St. Martin's Griffin
New York

This is a work of fiction. All of the characters, organizations, and events portrayed in this novel are either products of the author's imagination or are used fictitiously.

 Printed in the United States of America. For information, address St. Martin's Press, 175 Fifth Avenue, New York, N.Y. 10010.

www.stmartins.com

Library of Congress Cataloging-in-Publication Data

Nathan, Amy Sue.
The good neighbor : a novel / Amy Sue Nathan. — First edition.
pages ; cm
ISBN 978-1-250-04858-5 (trade paperback)
ISBN 978-1-4668-4955-6 (e-book)
1. Divorced women—Fiction. 2. Man-woman relationships—Fiction. I. Title.
PS3614.A85G66 2015
813'.6—dc23
2015019395

Our books may be purchased in bulk for promotional, educational, or business use. Please contact your local bookseller or the Macmillan Corporate and Premium Sales Department at (800) 221-7945, extension 5442, or by e-mail at MacmillanSpecialMarkets@macmillan.com.

First Edition: October 2015

10 9 8 7 6 5 4 3 2 1

For Zachary and Chloe, my superheroes.
I love watching you fly.

In memory of Souder Street.

You can never go home again, but the truth is you can never leave home, so it's all right.

—Maya Angelou

— Chapter 1 —

The Banana Song

THE DOORBELL RANG AND I knew it was my ex, just like when my lip tingled and I knew it was a cold sore. Most Wednesday nights I was ready for my midweek parenting respite. Not tonight. Tonight I longed for a snafu in Bruce's plans—a flat tire, a meeting, a hangnail. So tonight he was twenty minutes early. Of course.

Even so, I sang, "Daddy's here," and scooped Noah's toys from the kitchen table, shoving them inside his Spider-Man backpack along with two dinosaur books. I tucked in Spidey briefs and a clean sweatshirt, smoothing it hard as if to mark my territory.

My stomach rumbled and I slid my hand to my belly. Hollow gurgles akin to pregnancy flutters skittered across my palm. I smiled, remembering the moment I'd felt those first movements from Noah. I loved every one of them, even as they became an elbow in my ribs or a foot on my bladder.

I gathered the last of the boystuff, combed my fingers through my hair, and opened the front door. I left the storm door closed and wrangled Noah into his coat, hat, and mittens, which he plucked off. He reached up and touched my cheeks with his still-soft hands. I crouched down so we were nose to nose. I smelled apple juice, soap, and a hint of boy.

"See ya later, alligator!" he said, accenting the last syllable.

"In a while, crocodile!"

Noah linked his arms behind my neck and I stood. His legs dangled and his chest bounced with giggles. What would it be like when he was taller than me, taller than everyone, like Bruce? I was grateful, with a mother's longing, that he still had a round, soft face and fine, almost-black hair.

I nodded at my ex. Noah pushed out the door and hugged his dad with a force that landed Bruce against the metal railing. He kissed the top of Noah's head and held him at arm's length, as though memorizing the details. Bruce loved Noah like I did. That was something I still counted on, something I was grateful for. Something I needed to remember.

"Where's Amber?" Noah asked. His *r*'s sounded like *l*'s.

"Amber's in the car, buddy. She can't wait to see you."

My world had seized the moment I realized I was sharing Noah with someone other than Bruce. One day I watched my small child look up at Amber and reach for her hand. He smiled at her, and her meek grin widened. Amber took his hand in hers and patted it. I was awestruck. Or maybe dumbstruck. I was not surprised Amber warmed to Noah. That part I understood. But I was surprised how easily he reached for her. He held out his hand. He trusted her. He was a little boy who needed to be safe and happy and included. Yet instead of feeling a rush of gratitude and a momentary freedom from responsibilities, I burned, singed by an unlikely betrayal. Did he call her Mommy by mistake—or worse, not by mistake? Get a grip, I'd told myself. Bruce will have many more Ambers. Then I realized, for Noah's sake, that I didn't want that either.

Noah shot imaginary webs from his palms and Bruce fell back with a flourish. He ughed and arghed and begged Spider-Man to release him, but his performance was flat. Bruce sounded constrained, without enthusiasm. This was not his best trapped-dad voice.

"If Spider-Man lets me out of this web, I'll drop him off at school in the morning."

"Okeydoke," I said, instead of *No shit*. Bruce had been doing Thursday-morning drop-offs since school started in September.

"Smells delicious in there, Iz. If you're making your lasagna, he must be *some guy*."

I closed the door and leaned my back against it. Why did Bruce mention familiar details—my hair, an old sweater, the smell of lasagna? Didn't leaving mean he could no longer lay claim to these things? It was harder to forget, harder to forgive, when he kept poking into the past and pushing it forward. I shook my head to scatter the thoughts, then scurried to the kitchen knowing "some guy" was really "the girls," and they would be on time. My veggie lasagna would not be. It was bubbling on the sides, but soft and runny in the middle.

My lasagna brought me comfort. Moving "back home" had brought me comfort, too. And a little bit of shame. You grow up, move out, go to college, work, get married. You do not move back home with your small child in tow. Unless you need to. And I had—so I did.

Though I arrived months ago, I was still making the transition from living in the house-where-I-grew-up to living in that house as the only grown-up. But I was getting there. A moment of optimism blew through me, like a sigh of relief from the universe.

Still, lasagna from scratch was ambitious on a school night. Maybe I should have nuked a pizza on one of those silver crisping trays, opened a bag of Caesar salad, and squeezed dressing from a tube. Or ordered in. Who was I kidding? I, Izzy Lane, did not order in when the girls were coming for dinner. Even on a Wednesday.

Jade and Rachel arrived at the same time. Rachel leapt to hug me before she even closed the front door. Rachel moved the way she did throughout our childhood, as if she were Tinker Bell—just now with hips that swayed from the weight of four children under seven.

Jade looked up from her phone and surveyed the scene, her arms crossed, her foot tapping.

Rachel and Jade connected only through me. Opposite in demeanor and appearance, they were my perfect fit. Rachel's bounce balanced Jade's stillness. Jade's urban vibe muted Rachel's suburban air. I was a little like each of them, except they reveled in the lives they'd built from scratch. I loved them—despite their contentment.

I went to the kitchen and returned with a bottle of wine.

"We haven't done a Wednesday dinner in ages," Jade said. "What's up?"

"Can't I just make dinner for my two best friends when Noah's with Bruce?"

"No," they said in unison.

Rachel sat on the arm of the chair I still referred to as "Dad's." She tapped her fingers in sequence, from pinkie to pointer. One two three four, one two three four, one two three four. Over and over, as if she were waiting for something—and that something wasn't wine.

"I can't stand it anymore," she said.

"Stand what?"

"When are you going to tell us?"

"Tell you what?"

Rachel exploded with the fervor of a pageant toddler on Pixy Stix. "About Mac!"

"Mac?" Jade asked.

"How do you know about Mac?" I asked, dumbfounded. And maybe even a little dumb.

"Oh, come on, Izzy. You know I've been reading your blog! And so have all the girls at mahj."

"Her blog?" This was Jade. This was Jade getting annoyed. "Why am I the last to know these things?"

"I told you about it. . . ." I put my hands on my hips, a vague gesture of self-defense. "I didn't make a big deal about it, but I did tell you."

"She's right, Jade. She did. She started it the day Bruce moved out. But she calls herself Bizzy, remember?"

"That's what you did when Bruce left? Turned to your computer and made up an alias?"

"No, not exactly," I said, although—yes. Exactly. "It was just, well, I needed an outlet. Some sort of journal." And to be someone else. Someone whose world wasn't upside down and inside out. I was also someone else who didn't realize her first cousin had been taking notes.

Rachel's hands moved as if she were conducting a symphony. "When you wrote about the date where the guy squirted ketchup all over his eggs and how you had to clean off the lid of the ketchup bottle when he went to the men's room? It hit me. No one enjoys cleaning dirty ketchup lids like a Lane."

Rachel should know.

"Jade, you should see the comments! There are tons of them."

Jade perked up. *Tons of comments* had gotten her attention.

"She's totally an advice goddess. Izzy told one woman to stop trying to be someone she wasn't, because then the right guy wouldn't be able to find her. That's genius, right?"

It *was* good advice. Why was I surprised? Though I'd never thought of my master's in school counseling as a boon to my blogging escapades before, it was.

"It's true, the advice I give seems to be helpful to people. But some of the stories I've told aren't exactly . . ."

"They're awesome! Tell Jade about your dates."

"Dates? You've gone on more dates? I thought you said it 'wasn't the right time.' " Jade used air quotes. Jade hated air quotes.

"When it's the right person, it's always the right time," Rachel said. "Tell Jade about Mac!"

"Who's Mac?" Now Jade crossed her arms.

"Her boyfriend!"

No. I was not telling anyone about Mac.

"You have a boyfriend?" Jade stood and went to the closet. She took out her coat and draped it over her arm. "I worry about you every weekend when you say you're doing nothing, when you won't meet me in town, and now I find out you're really out tooling around the city with a man you're keeping a secret? Oh my God. Is he married?"

That's what she thinks of me? "I am not tooling around with anyone!"

"Okay, so you don't want to call him your boyfriend." Rachel grinned. "But you're seeing someone. Mac is amazing. From everything Izzy told me—well, she didn't tell me, really—he's smart and funny and handsome. She met him on JDate—"

"Stop!" I yelled. "He's not what you think. It's not what it seems."

Rachel put her hands over her ears. "Please! I don't want to hear it. Let your old married cousin live vicariously through you a little longer." She grabbed me again. "Nobody's perfect, you know."

Rachel was wrong. Mac *was* perfect. Mac was perfect because I'd invented him—all six two of him, with his full head of dark hair, his humble upbringing, his self-made career. What was his career again? Did he have one? I wasn't sure. Oops. But more important than any career was that Mac was devoted to me. Of course he was. He was my cyber version of *Weird Science*.

Mac had appeared just in the nick of time, on a Saturday morning in October. Amber and Bruce had shown up at Noah's soccer game in matching Temple Owls sweatshirts. Stupid matching sweatshirts. The blatant coupledom punched me in the gut. I had always wanted to be a matchy-matchy couple, but not Bruce. I had bought us matching Phillies T-shirts and caps one Hanukkah, but he refused to wear his when I wore mine. The Hanna Andersson striped pajamas I ordered for us *and* Noah, the ones in which I imagined we'd look like a catalog family, stayed folded and bagged. Then Noah grew, Bruce moved out, and I got a full refund.

Bruce and Amber's sweatshirts, in Temple's official cherry and white, were crisp and new, yet worn. Nonrefundable.

They sat in front of me, our usual effort to appear united. We exchanged our tactical greeting: Bruce took Noah's duffel bag; I reminded him about the cosmic bowling party that afternoon, and decorating the sukkah at the synagogue the next day.

"I know. We'll be there," Bruce said. Amber nodded. They refocused on the field and leaned into each other's shoulder.

We'll be there? Since when were *they* a *we*?

"I'll be there, too," I said. "But now I've got to go. I have plans with . . ." Who on earth did I have plans with? "My boyfriend."

I could have said I had a report to finish or that I was having lunch with Rachel. I could have offered nothing more than good-bye. But I didn't because it wasn't enough. I wasn't enough. I wasn't a *we.* I was a *me.* A *me, myself, and I.* And I was alone, laden with inadequacy. Embarrassment filled me. The matching sweatshirts had been my tipping point and I'd invented a boyfriend. So what?

Back then, the mere façade of moving forward had left me aglow.

Tonight my cheeks burned with embarrassment.

"Well, I have to tell you, I'm relieved," Jade said.

"Excuse me?"

"I thought you were going to say you were getting back together with Bruce."

I leapt toward Jade and hugged her. "Really?"

Did she know something I didn't?

"I had no idea why you invited us here. Just coming for dinner on a Wednesday seemed a little unusual, Pea, I've got to be honest." Jade threw her phone into her oversize pocketbook. She used the nickname she'd given me at Penn the day our freshman English professor anointed us *two peas in a pod*. "You hole up here, in this house, and never leave except for work. Yes, you take care of Noah. Yes, you go to work every day. But that's all you do. And then you invite us over on a Wednesday night when I know it's the only night you have to yourself."

All I had wanted was company for dinner, a glass of wine, a few belly laughs. "I am so sorry you're worried about me." I swallowed air. Rachel would have to live her romantic dream through someone else. "There's more."

Rachel clasped her hands. "You're in love!"

"No!"

She whispered, "Pregnant?"

"No!"

"Then what?"

Keep it light. No big deal. It's all a phase. Like Pilates.

"Mac isn't exactly how he seems."

"Is anyone?" Jade asked.

In real life I hoped the answer was yes.

"Just enjoy yourself," Jade continued. "But I want to hear more about this little blog of yours, missy!" She dug out her phone, tapped, and scrolled. "There, got it! The *Bizzy Blog*. Very cute." She held it up, showcasing a miniature version of my make-believe life.

"It gets . . . well, it got, a few thousand hits. Per day." This was true. I worked to keep my smile in check. "Apparently, I'm good at it." They were not the most important words, but hearing them aloud reminded me that the blog had served a purpose. I had created something that connected me to others. And it was mine. It belonged only to me. My thoughts and words were not like dishes or towels or dining-room chairs, or even a five-year-old boy.

No one could leave and then claim half.

Rachel and Jade stared at each other, then at me, then back at each other. I often felt them vying for top branch in my confidante tree, but now I sensed a kinship between them.

"The thing is, though—I mean, the issue is—Mac's not real." There. I said it. I stood, ready to purge my reasons for embellishing my life and manufacturing men, and more important, for not telling them any of it.

"It's fine," Jade said. "I get it."

"You do?"

"Mac's not his real name. And he probably doesn't know you're writing about him. Bloggers do that all the time. Change names to protect the innocent, so to speak. So you made up a name and he doesn't know you write about him. No big deal."

"What's his real name? I want to Google him! Is he really a dentist?"

How had I forgotten that Mac was a dentist?

"Look, it's okay if you don't want to tell us his name for a while," Jade said. "I don't tell you everything either, especially about the men I date. It's just—*easier.* I think it's normal."

If this was normal, I was in big trouble. "Wait, you don't tell me everything?"

Jade just lifted her eyebrows and smirked. "No. So I guess we're even."

"All I care about is that you're happy," Rachel said.

I wanted her to make me accountable—or to encourage me to be accountable to myself. I wanted her to challenge me, fight me, but Rachel wasn't a fighter.

"Taking care of Noah by yourself, working, dating, and then you have this blog and you meet this *Mac* . . . it's easy to get caught up. I'm planning my reunion and I can spend hours online looking up classmates and sending e-mails. It sucks me right in. I lose all track of time. But I don't understand wanting to share your life with strangers more than with us."

It was easy to banter with strangers, sometimes more so than talking to my friends, or my brothers, or my parents. I had grown weary of my mother's rolled eyes and weak redirects when I talked about Bruce. I cringed at how some of my married friends thought it would be great to be single again. My brothers were compassionate, but wouldn't be caught dead *back home*. How many times could they listen to me say the same old thing? But sometimes the same old thing was all I had. Writing about it enabled me to make sense of the nonsensical. Plus, strangers had no expectations. They were patient. Even prodding. If they were bored, they were silent. If they rolled their eyes, I couldn't see. To me, the words adhered to the virtual page as new, and without consequence.

I knew nothing of search engines or keywords or that "A Bad Date with a Defense Attorney" would result in hundreds of hits and rampant advice about finding a new lawyer.

But apparently some folks actually *read* the post and commented about real-life Paul the Deviant DA, the perfect-on-paper Jewish lawyer who brought me an erotic novel on our second date because I'd said I liked to read. The people who chimed in on that post were keepers—unlike Mr. Shifty Shades.

My readers didn't feel like strangers. They were people who helped me forget about Bruce and divorce and moving back home. They were the ones who cheered me on when I wrote about blurting out "Mac" at the soccer field. Of course, I'd left out the part about making him up. I'd intended to be honest, but the truth slipped out of my fingers like Noah's green slime. And it was just as messy.

Rachel stepped closer to me. It wasn't my intention to hurt her feelings. My intention was to safeguard my own.

She twirled her fingers in her short brown curls. Rachel twirled her body when she was happy, her hair when she was not.

"Well, no matter what his real name is, we don't have

to worry so much now that you have someone to talk to at night, someone to spend time with when Noah's with Bruce. Someone who knows how great you are. Besides us, I mean. Right?" Rachel looked at Jade.

"Absolutely."

I could've tried again, tried harder, but at that moment, I just didn't want to. Perhaps they didn't really want to know that I'd conjured up Mac because seeing Bruce with Amber had brought me to my emotional knees. I was sure they didn't want to know I sometimes slept in Noah's bed when he was with Bruce, or on the sofa when Noah was home, because a queen-size bed, with its space for two, was overwhelming.

Jade and Rachel loved me, but they hadn't let me explain. Worse, they had rearranged my words to meet their needs. I got it. The lie was much prettier than the truth.

But enough was enough.

Maybe it was time to exert damage control by pressing the little button on the dashboard that said DELETE FOREVER. Then my words would evaporate, Times Roman letters scattering chaotically. "The blog was really just an experiment. For fun. I'm deleting it. I don't need a bunch of strangers knowing my business. You're right."

"Don't you dare! Don't abandon your readers when they've started to trust you. It took me months for Pop Philly to get that many hits per day." It had tens of thousands now.

Jade's phone buzzed. She tapped the screen with her forefinger and scrolled. "Damn. I've got to go. I'm a little crazed lately."

And I'm a liar dating a make-believe man named after my laptop.

"You didn't eat!"

Jade grabbed a handful of Goldfish crackers out of a bowl. "Seafood."

Rachel headed for the Goldfish, too.

"Rache, stay!"

"No, you'll have the whole night to yourself. Seth doesn't like putting the kids to bed anyway."

I had the whole night to myself every Wednesday. Every other weekend I was on my own. I didn't need, or want, any more alone time. That was another reason I dove online every night after Noah went to sleep—companionship on a whim and a click. Another reason for Mac.

"What is so important that you have to leave right now?" I shifted my effort to Jade, but she guffawed.

"You're not the only one with secrets."

Chapter 2

Pick-Up Sticks

I WRAPPED MY HANDS around the mug of chamomile tea and lowered my face to the brim. Mrs. Feldman appeared to be waiting for an answer to a question she hadn't asked. I felt ten again. Maybe twelve.

I'd sat in this kitchen when I was a young girl, when the appliances were harvest gold and the beverage was orange Kool-Aid, which had left triangle-shaped stains on the sides of my mouth that I liked to pretend were fangs. When Mrs. Feldman served hot chocolate, I had always burnt my tongue reaching for a clump of cocoa at the bottom. I'd eaten pounds of butter cookies from a tin, my favorite being the ones with the cherry in the middle. I'd done homework in this kitchen on many afternoons when my brothers were working alongside our parents at the hardware store.

Now, almost thirty years later, I was in Mrs. Feldman's house again, and for the same reason. No one was at home waiting for me.

"So, that didn't turn out the way you planned, did it?" Mrs. Feldman's hands quivered as she refolded an embroidered cloth napkin.

I imagined she was making a tulip or a swan, but it ended up more like a pocket. She slid her spoon into the opening.

"I don't care what Jade said. I'm going to delete the blog when I get home." I stood up from the table and added three servings of lasagna to Mrs. Feldman's freezer. I placed another on the top shelf of the fridge. I would check in a few days to see if she'd eaten any of them.

"You'll feel better once you straighten this out. You should go home and call them. But no texting. It's too impersonal."

"I'll talk to Jade later. And I'll call Rachel tomorrow."

"You can go home now and do it."

"No, Jade's working and Rachel goes to bed right after her kids. Anyway, I like being here with you." I liked that one person knew everything.

"And I have a freezer full of lasagna to prove it!" Geraldine Feldman may have been eighty-five, but she rolled her eyes like a teenager.

I folded my napkin, but only came up with what looked like—a folded napkin.

"You should have seen the looks on their faces. Rachel was bursting at the seams thinking I'd been on a lot of dates and had a boyfriend; it didn't even seem to register when I said he wasn't real. Like she didn't even hear me. Jade was preoccupied with work, as usual, relieved I wasn't getting back together with Bruce. Oh, and that apparently I wasn't the shut-in she thought I was."

"If they only knew most of your date nights were with *me*!"

I threw my napkin across the table. Mrs. Feldman laughed and handed it back to me with a little finger twirl that meant "keep folding."

"That whole Mac thing. What was I thinking?"

"You were thinking it was easier to be alone if no one thought you were alone."

"Do you want more tea? Dessert? I brought Jell-O in those little plastic cups."

"Don't change the subject, Elizabeth." Mrs. Feldman did not believe in nicknames. "What's done is done. Tell those friends of yours once and for all that you invented a man because it hurt too much to see Bruce with another woman. And that this helped a little."

"That's not true." It didn't help at all. "I just got a little carried away."

"Getting a little carried away can get you into a lot of trouble."

I didn't want a lecture. I wanted dessert. I stood and cleared the table, washed the dishes with hot, soapy water, then placed them into the dishwasher to be *sanitized*. If I didn't do it right, Mrs. Feldman would unload, wash, and reload after I'd left.

The whole point of my being here was so she didn't do all that work. (Well, in the beginning that was the whole point.) I'd promised my parents and Mrs. Feldman's son, Ray, that I would look in on her. It wasn't hard. Mrs. Feldman and I galloped right back into our pattern of codependence, as if I were six. I knew she needed me now, but looking back on it, she must have needed me then, too. Why else would she have spent hours with me when she could have filled her own empty nest with canasta and committee meetings?

I refilled Mrs. Feldman's mug with hot water and sat down at the table with my lukewarm tea. She stared out the kitchen window and sighed. I sighed in reply.

"It's not the same as it used to be, but it's home."

As quick as a hiccup, it was no longer about me. Perhaps it never was. I nodded to the rhythm of Mrs. Feldman's silence. It was dark outside, but the streetlights meant it was never too dark to see Good Street with its parallel-parked cars jammed onto both sides of the narrow road. I was lucky my old neighborhood hadn't fallen into complete disrepair when I'd arrived, divorced and slightly mortified, on my parents' doorstep in July. I hadn't planned for my childhood home to become Noah's. I hadn't planned for a lot of things. The house had been languishing on the market for two years, thanks to the economic downturn. So when I moved in, my parents were able to take their IRAs and Social Security to Margate, just three blocks from their favorite South Jersey beach, and right next door to their dreams. They got their new home and I got their—my?—old one. I adopted their second mortgage payments, Dad's chair, and Mom's houseplants, which had since gone to ficus and dieffenbachia heaven.

I had mastered the nuances of redbrick row-house living by the time I was six. So would Noah. I spent my childhood running up and jumping down these cement steps, playing Barbies and jacks on crowded patios. I'd played wallball on every wall and stepball on every step. I'd memorized the insides of my neighbors' homes and lives. It was more like an urban commune than one block in the center of a middle-class Northeast Philadelphia neighborhood. I didn't know if all streets had been like my street. *My street*. Two words that had filled up my childhood heart.

I laid my hand atop Mrs. Feldman's, her knuckles jutting against skin that was smooth as hand-washed silk.

She returned to the kitchen from wherever she had been beyond her gaze. She looked at me and smiled. "It'll be okay, Elizabeth."

I didn't know if she meant for her or for me. Or for us both.

In the living room we settled onto the sofa, cups in hand. Mrs. Feldman had eliminated the clear plastic slipcovers in the nineties, and updated the style then, too, but not since. The décor was dated and lush, mixed with IKEA particleboard in varying shades of neutral. Some things old and some things new. It all suited her—and it suited me when I was here. I dusted the bookshelves and tchotchkes. She nagged me to stop as she pointed around the room at spots that I'd missed: on top of the magazines, beneath the lampshade, under a wooden box that looked like a kitschy souvenir pirate's treasure chest and was locked, perhaps sealed, a ruse against tourists.

I feigned the need for the bathroom and gave it a one-minute scrubbing—a squirt of toilet cleaner that had been left on the floor, a swish of a paper towel (a brand-new roll) damp with disinfectant under the seat and on all the knobs and handles. A cleaning service came every week, but Mrs. Feldman's had always been spit-spot and ready for company. If I didn't do this, she would.

After my surreptitious clean, which Mrs. Feldman was well

aware of, I'd watch TV with her until nine, as I had almost every Wednesday night since July.

"Hand me the clicker," she said. "Do you know I remember the first time you brought Bruce home to meet your parents?"

This was a walk down memory lane I did not want to take. "And you were knocking on our door within two minutes." I waggled my finger. "You pretended you didn't know we were there." Why did she always have to bring up Bruce?

"He was very handsome. And tall. Tall Jewish men are not a dime a dozen, you know. Even your brothers aren't that tall."

"I know."

"You had such a beautiful wedding."

"Yep." The one my parents had taken out a second mortgage to pay for. The one I was paying off. Paying back. Paying for, in more ways than one.

"We all thought you two were perfect together."

"We were wrong."

My cell phone rang. I let it go to voice mail. Then it rang again. I let it go to voice mail. It started buzzing again right away.

"Hello?"

"Where are you?"

I mouthed, *Bruce,* to Mrs. Feldman, and she ambled to the kitchen to give me privacy I didn't need. "What's wrong?"

"Are you home?"

"No."

"Your car is here."

"Where are you?"

"Double-parked."

"Where?"

"Outside your house."

I walked to the window, and there he was. Idle. Expectant. "What's wrong?"

"Are you alone?"

Bruce stepped out of the car, dipped into the backseat, and, as if by magic, appeared carrying Noah.

"No, Bruce, I'm not alone. Is Noah okay?"

"He's fine. Does Mrs. Feldman have a key so we can get in?"

I clicked off my phone as the doorbell rang. Mrs. Feldman answered it before I could stop her. The peril of living in a narrow row house was that it didn't take long to get from point A or point B to the front door. I glanced at the mirror behind the sofa. I jostled my fingers under and through my hair, smoothed my sweater over my long, still-narrow torso. In walked Bruce. In bounced Noah, more like Tigger than Spider-Man. He and Bruce were catawampus and disheveled.

"Daddy has a meeting so I need to come hooome!" Noah wiggled, and Bruce set him on the floor in his pajamas. And socks. In January.

"Say hello to Mrs. Feldman, Noah."

"Hello, Mrs. Feldman." Bruce kissed her on the cheek. I knew that when he wasn't looking, she'd wipe it off with one of her napkins.

"Noah, come to the kitchen for a little nosh." Bruce followed. "No nosh for you." She pointed to the chair and Bruce sat. The power of the eighty-five-year-old index finger.

Noah ran over and hugged his surrogate grandmother. She kissed him on the head.

"Daddy has a meeting in the morning," Noah repeated, to make sure Mommy heard. He skipped to the kitchen, Mrs. Feldman following.

"You said you're not home and this is where you are?" Bruce looked around the living room and toward the kitchen and dining room.

"I'm not home, Bruce. This"—I opened my arms to the side—"is not where I live."

"You said you weren't alone."

"I wasn't alone. I was watching TV with Mrs. Feldman." Now he knew I hadn't had a man over for dinner, or if I had, that it had been a bust. "And earlier, Jade and Rachel came for dinner." Why did I give him information he didn't ask for? Bad habits were hard to break.

"And here I thought I was going to meet your mysterious guy. What's his name? Oh, right. Mac."

"Who's Mac?"

I whipped around, startled. Noah stood at the entrance to the living room, Mrs. Feldman's arm around him. Noah's mouth was full of cookie. Or Jell-O. Or both, by the look of his chipmunk cheeks.

Mrs. Feldman patted Noah's shoulder. "Sweetie, don't talk with your mouth full."

Back in my house, Bruce stood in the foyer with his feet apart, digging them in, as if he were trying to create indelible footprints in the new Berber carpet. He bounced a bit. "Great padding."

"You didn't bring Noah home to assess the carpet in my living room. What's going on?"

"I got called into a meeting at nine in New York. I need to be on the seven a.m. train, which means I'll leave at six if I'm going to have time to stop for coffee."

His words entered a section of my brain I'd reserved for Bruce blather. I couldn't care less about the logistics of his workday—not anymore. Yet he told me these things often, maybe as filler, maybe to hear his own voice, maybe because it didn't occur to him that there was anyone who didn't care what he did or said. But I did care that he was bailing on Noah and rearranging our arrangement.

"Fine, whatever. But next time you are summoned on a *Noah day,* remind them that you are a divorced father with moral and *legal* obligations."

Bruce scrunched his eyebrows together and looked as if he were trying to remember if he'd turned off the stove or left on the iron. Was I talking gibberish or had he simply tuned me out?

"What if I had gone away *overnight*?" But we both knew the answer.

I'd have come home.

— *Chapter 3* —

Red Light, Green Light

GOOD PARKING KARMA MEANT good karma in general, so when I pulled into an open parking spot on 12th Street—before eight o'clock on a Saturday evening, yet—I knew I'd made the right decision begging Jade to meet me for dinner and drinks. I'd convince her Mac was imaginary, spend the night at her house, we'd do Sunday brunch at Sabrina's Café, and I'd spend the day with Jade being a single woman in the city. Not a single mom. Not an ex-wife. Not a guidance counselor, a daughter, or a sister. And *not* a blogger, though technically, I still was one. Bruce's change of plans and my overbooked days at Liberty High School interfered with *my* plan to disband the blog. I had allowed my *Bizzy Blog* to stagnate over the past week and a half and it was still getting traffic, even with no new content, even though I wished the whole thing away. Maybe while the blog was on hold, I'd move forward and forget about it and my imaginary boyfriend.

I was very ready for this night with a *real* friend. I pushed aside the thoughts of cyber everything, ex-husband anything, and decided I'd pay for a round of something pink with a high alcohol content. Maybe tonight I'd even meet someone real or Jade would fix me up and I'd never have to sign up for an online dating site again. I knew that would be too easy, but it was fun to think about something being easy for once.

My phone buzzed. Bruce Silverstein was a pain in the neck. This was BS, indeed.

"It took you long enough." I'd left Bruce a message the day before.

"Mommy?"

"Oh, hi, honey." I raised my voice an octave and added *always answer the phone sweetly* to my mental to-do list. "Getting ready for bed?"

"Amber is making me a smoothie, but Daddy wants to talk to you."

Of course he does. I left a message at a reasonable time, on a reasonable day. He calls back the one weekend night I decide to go into Center City.

"Okeydoke. I'll see you tomorrow night. Love you."

"Love you, too."

I heard scuffling and then I heard Bruce clear his throat.

"Did you straighten out the credit-card mix-up?" I asked. "Was it really necessary for the day-care director to tell me my ex-husband's card on file was declined? She said she left you messages."

"I know."

"Tell me you straightened this out."

"Not exactly."

"What do you mean *not exactly*?" I was leaning against the

car now, like I did on Good Street in the summers when I watched the big kids play stickball in the middle of the street. Now I watched couples navigating mounds of grime-speckled snow left over from the last storm.

"I wasn't going to mention anything yet, but Amber said I should."

"And eight o'clock on a Saturday night is when Amber told you to do this? You're getting mighty compliant in your old age, Bruce." Bruce had turned forty last year and had not been convinced it was the new thirty.

"Look, I'm just trying to do what's right. Do you want to hear this or not?"

"Yes."

"My card was declined because I didn't have enough in my account to cover the charge."

"Obviously."

"I lost my job, Iz."

I lurched forward, half lying on the hood of the car, which was still warm. I blinked and blinked, light flashing in front of my eyes, a strobe of sadness, confusion, and anger. What would we do? Would he be okay? How dare they! He works so hard! He has a family! "Oh my God, Bruce, I'm so sorry." I whispered.

Then I remembered. It wasn't my job to console him; that role was no longer mine.

I covered my eyes with my hand to make myself invisible. It worked for babies. Why not adults?

I knew what this was really about. "You still have to pay for day care, Bruce. You have an obligation to Noah." And to me.

"I'll do my best."

"It's not like I buy champagne and bonbons with that money, Bruce, so go get another job!" I knew it wasn't that easy, but spit the words anyway. "You sell drugs, for God's sake. Go sell them somewhere else." A young couple stopped and stared. "Pharmaceuticals," I mouthed. "Prescription drugs."

"I said I'd do my best."

I stomped my foot so hard that a pain shot through to my knee. I uncovered my eyes and checked the bottom of my boot, making sure I hadn't broken the heel. "When did you find out?" I waited for him to say "Yesterday."

"About a month ago."

I had ignored the signs. The messy appearance. Showing up early. Even this past Wednesday I figured he'd just taken the day off. Apparently he'd been "off" for a long time.

"What about your emergency meeting in New York?"

"It was an interview. Didn't work out."

Did anything?

"What's the point of this call, Bruce? Just to ruin my night?"

"I thought you should know I don't know when I'll be able to pay for day care, or to send the next check, but I'll try."

"Are you kidding me? You'll try? What are we supposed to do in the meantime?"

"We'll all just have to cut back. I have a few irons in the fire, and they've tied up most of my cash. As it is, I'm just going to squeak by paying my own mortgage and car payments."

"Not my problem, Bruce." But it was.

"Maybe Mrs. Feldman can watch Noah," Bruce sputtered. "He loves her. Didn't you stay with her when you were little?"

"Mrs. Feldman is eighty-five!" Bruce was impervious to everyone's limitations except his own.

"Maybe your parents can help."

My parents were two hours away and Bruce knew it. "I know. Now that you're not working, you can take Noah to school and pick him up every day. You can even stay at my house until I get home. If you have an interview, schedule it during school hours."

"That's another thing I wanted to talk to you about."

What now?

"I'm not going to be here for a while."

"What do you mean you're not going to be here?"

"I'm going to Palo Alto."

"California? You have a son, Bruce. He belongs to both of us. Not just to me and not just to you when you feel like it. You can't leave him." Or me again. I willed myself to not throw up in the middle of the street, or on top of my car.

"Stop!" he yelled. I pictured Noah alarmed. Bruce was not a yeller. Even the end of our marriage was met with quiet conversations and sticky-note messages on the refrigerator. "It's only for a few weeks. Amber's company is based there."

My head swirled. A few weeks and I was supposed to feel grateful? I didn't like being away from Noah for a weekend, and Bruce was leaving for a few weeks and used the word *only*? And *Amber's company*—where did I even start with that one? "You need to look for a job, Bruce. You don't get to go on a vacation with your girlfriend. You don't get to go on a vacation, period."

"Amber is giving me airline miles, and obviously I'll stay

with her in a company apartment. I'll spend less there than I would at home. And I'll be doing a lot of networking."

"Oh, is that what they're calling it now? I must have missed the memo."

"It's only three weeks. A month at most," he mumbled. "We'll talk on the phone and you can hook up a Web chat. Noah understands."

"He doesn't understand. He's *five*. I've got to go." I walked down 12th Street to turn left onto Sansom toward the restaurant. Meema's was Jade's hip hangout du jour. It served designer cocktails and gourmet comfort food. Whatever that was.

"Izzy?"

"What now, Bruce?"

"I'm sorry."

I wouldn't let his sincere tone fool me again. "I scramble to make ends meet and you lie on the beach. You're such a man, Bruce." I knew what got to him and was glad to use it, even though I had always promised myself I'd play fair.

"First, Palo Alto is near San Francisco. I'm not going to be lying on the beach. Second, I'm just asking you to deal with this for a month or two."

"Are you kidding me? You do know I'm calling my lawyer. You have to pay child support, Bruce. You have to pay for day care. I'm pretty sure that going to California indefinitely would be considered abandonment. Way to help Noah rack up the therapy bills before he's six."

"Do you really want Noah to get caught up in a court battle?" Bruce knew what got to me. "I promise I'll make it right.

I would never let Noah down, I just need a little time. I know what you think of me, but I'm a great dad, Izzers."

How dare he use the nickname for my nickname. He was playing on my emotions, my sympathy, the kind heart that he knew existed beneath the one he'd turned to stone.

I stopped at the entrance to Meema's, but didn't remember walking there. "I've got to go." I pulled open the door. Out sailed a line of revelers.

Now I looked like a doorman and a doormat.

"Will you give me a chance to turn this around before you take me to court?"

"I'll think about it."

"I'll have Noah home tomorrow night at six. Unless you want an extra night off since . . ."

"No. Stick to the schedule." I wanted my boy to come home.

"Iz?"

"What?"

"I know it's a lot to ask, but please trust me."

I had trusted him more than once, and that didn't work out so well. All I could do was push END.

— Chapter 4 —

Kerplunk

MEEMA'S WAS CROWDED AND dimly lit. I looked to the bar and saw blurry faces, bodies moving in slow motion. What was I doing here? Who was I there to see? I gazed above shoulders and heads and saw one graceful arm waving back and forth. Right. Jade. I weaved through the pretty people, none of whom resembled anyone in my real life. They lined up like bowling pins as they waited for tables and cocktails and lovers and friends. Their faces revealed no outward worry. Were they all as happy as they seemed? How I wished I hadn't answered the phone so I could seem happy, too.

I stepped in front of Jade and grabbed her arm.

Her eyes opened wide. "What's wrong, Pea?"

"Everything." I burst into tears.

Jade grabbed her drink and draped her arm over my shoulder. Then she took my coat and handed it to the man standing next to her. He looked familiar but I couldn't place the face, so I just nodded. Let him have the coat. My self-esteem was in the pocket with some coins and a straw wrapper. He could have it all. I didn't care.

"Let's go somewhere," Jade said. And by *somewhere* she meant *inside* the ladies' lounge.

She nudged me onto a chair and plucked tissues from the deluxe cozy-covered box near the sinks. Then she scooted next to me and dabbed my eyes. "Waterproof mascara. Good choice. Now tell me what's wrong. Is it Mac?"

"No. Bruce lost his job."

Jade stared, waiting for more. Wasn't that enough?

"He bailed on the day-care bill and I have no idea if he'll pay support next month!" The ominous uncertainty drained any feeling from my legs. "And he asked me to give him time to get back on his feet. Can you believe that?"

Jade nodded. The woman at the sink raised her eyebrows at me in solidarity before turning on the water.

"It's a bad economy."

"Excuse me?"

"I'm sorry, but is it really your problem that Bruce needs a new job?"

"Yes, it's my problem." I grabbed the tissues from her hand. I would wipe my own tears and snot. How could I expect her to understand? I might have been Queen of Chicken Nuggets and School District Paperwork, but Jade was Center City's social media sweetheart.

"I'm sorry. I didn't realize. I thought moving back home made things easier for you."

Back home. That stung like a school-yard pinch. "It does. But easier still doesn't mean easy. Anyway, just because I can take care of everything on my own doesn't mean I should have to. It's his obligation. Noah is his kid, too. And with Bruce's support added to my salary, I don't really struggle to pay the bills. We're okay. Now I'll pinch pennies and he'll lie on the beach. He's going to California with Amber."

Now I had her attention. Or not. Jade nodded like a television therapist. "He's moved on." She rubbed my back in circles. "At this point, he's supposed to. You should be moving on, too. I thought you had. Or at least that you were trying."

"This has nothing to do with Bruce and Amber, it has to do with Bruce leaving when he should be here helping with Noah. And taking care of us—not leaving us again." I gasped after hearing my words aloud.

"Déjà vu, Pea."

She was right. Bruce had left me flailing at critical moments through the nine years I'd known him. It was the times he *didn't* that had made me believe I could count on him. I realized now he acted out of obligation, in deference to his good-guy image. If after his leaving, the obligation vanished for him, and the image vanished for me, then why did the disappointment feel the same? The hollow at the bottom of my stomach. The twinge in my side. Stress manifested itself in my gut every time.

"You're amazing, Pea. Remember that. I could *not* do what you're doing—working, raising a kid, seeing an ex *all* the time . . ."

"You would if you had to, honey." The voice drifted toward us from a bathroom stall.

Ladies' washrooms were peculiar gathering places. Strangers

shared toilet paper squares under stall dividers, divvied up tampons, and ensured no one left with a skirt tucked into her underwear or a bra strap showing—unless it was the style.

"But I'm still confused." Jade was never confused. She was meticulous and methodical. She was a problem solver. A puzzle lover. "I get why you're upset about Bruce going to California. Let's face it. That's just Bruce. At first, he does what's right for everyone. You know that. In the end, he just *can't* and he does what's right for him. Frankly, you should try it, but the Noah part . . ."

"I shouldn't have to support Noah on my own."

"Does it really make that much of a difference?"

"Yes. It's a lot of money. But if I go right to court, I'm still going to look like the bad guy."

"Then don't. Give Bruce a chance."

"Why are you defending him?"

"I'm not. I just want you to do what's right for you—not what you think Bruce *deserves*."

"So Noah has to be without his dad, we both have to be without the money we need, and Bruce can work on some scheme and pursue his passion out in California?"

"You never know when opportunity might come knocking on your door."

"As long as it's not Bruce knocking, I'll answer it."

Then a voice filtered out from another bathroom stall: "Good riddance to bad rubbish, honey."

Then the toilet flushed, which said it all.

Jade and I joined a group of mostly hipsters huddled around a small high top. Coat Guy was there, but no longer held my coat.

"Everyone! This is Elizabeth Lane," Jade said.

"Izzy," I said. I widened my eyes and smiled at Jade. I thought we were here to have a girls' night out, *girls* meaning *me and Jade,* not me and Jade and six twenty- or thirtysomethings, half of whom weren't girls. Not to mention Coat Guy, who looked my age, and who looked familiar. I leafed through my mental photo album of Jade's exes, many of whom she'd stayed friends with, but he didn't look like her type. My thoughts were then drowned out from the welcoming committee and its clutter of nice-to-meet-yous and we've-heard-so-much-about-yous.

"You want to help me out here?" I side-mouthed to Jade.

"This is my team," Jade said it as if that explained everything. "From Pop Philly."

"Oh." I shook hands fist over fist and made eye contact with each person, trying to match the person with the details I'd heard from Jade over the past two years. Since launching the online hub for all things interesting or new in the city, Jade had told me every time she hired someone, added a blog or an angle or a new design, the same way a mom rattled on about her baby's monthly milestones. I was supposed to be reading Pop Philly every day when really I popped in once a week. Or when I remembered. So maybe I didn't keep up with everything that was going on. But this—the hair, the smiles, the clothes, the piercings, the visible tattoos—it was all too much. They were all too young. None of them, except Coat Guy, were older than thirty. I'm sure they all felt my thirty-nine-year-old vibe before I'd merged onto I-95.

"So this is our *Philly over Forty* blogger, huh?"

My mouth dropped open and I looked at Jade, who pointed to her own mouth so I'd shut mine.

"Yes, Izzy is going to be the newest blogger for Pop Philly!"

My mouth opened again. What did Jade say? "I can't."

"Why not, honey?" Dreadlocks spoke up with a lilt in his voice, songlike, sweet. "I sent a link to your *Bizzy Blog* to my dad, and you know what? He'd already seen it! When AOL slaps your URL for a few hours on their home page, lots of people see it. And I didn't even know people still used AOL." A collective nod told me to delete my AOL account.

"Tell her what your dad said, Holden."

Holden. Dreadlocks=Holden.

"He says he's following your lead and moving forward. And my parents have been divorced for ten years."

Something I wrote gave a stranger confidence? Some posts had a lot of comments, but never close to the number of page views. I wondered what the lurkers thought, and now I knew. At least about one. Someone old enough to be Dreadlocks'—Holden's—father, was listening to my little words of wisdom? Wait, did this mean *I* was old enough to be Holden's mother?

"That's very nice, but I'm just not writing anymore." I counted in my head and figured Holden's dad must be much older than me.

"I think you owe it to your reading public," Nose Ring said. Aside from the tiny gold hoop that went in and out with her every word, this young woman looked like a Main Line prep school princess. She had blunt-cut, straight blond hair, naturally long lashes, and clavicles that looked like rolling hills. She also had a tattoo on the inside of her forearm, script I couldn't quite read at an upside-down and sideways angle. I peeked around at her feet, expecting stilettos, ballet flats, or pumps, but saw combat boots. And she saw me.

"I don't think I have a reading public."

"You had over eight thousand unique hits your first month," Jade said. "And once you're on Pop Philly, everyone who comes to the site will see your column because we're putting it on the landing page. It will also headline our social-scene page on Mondays and Fridays."

Jade's lingo was cluttering my clear thinking.

"We want to cater to a new demographic," Coat Guy said. Everyone nodded but no one introduced him.

"Drew's on point. And that's where you come in," Holden added.

Coat Guy=Drew. "Darby, tell Izzy what Jade and I explained to you."

Darby breathed deep. Her nose ring wiggled. Darby. "Singles in their forties are the fastest-growing demographic in the country, so we need to hook them. Then we need to keep them hooked." She flashed an orthodontic smile toward Drew, who looked old enough to be her father.

"You mean you want me to attract old people?"

Drew laughed. "I'm forty-two. Watch it."

Coat Guy, Drew, forty-two. He was a Dr. Seuss rhyme. *That* I could remember.

"And considering I'm hitting four-oh just a few months after you, it's definitely not old. Not for anything, least of all dating."

Jade lifted her glass and then sipped from her straw until the glass was empty. "I am going to the bar for a refill."

Darby held the table edge with two hands. She glanced at Drew, but fixed her gaze on me. Did she have a crush on him? That couldn't be right. "I was going to write this column in addition to my restaurant reviews. It was going to be like a promotion, but then Jade said not to worry about it, she had the perfect person for the job. So, fine. I think I could have totally appealed to an older audience, but she's the boss. And you're at the right age, I guess. And her best friend. So I guess that makes you perfect."

"Perfect? Who's perfect?" Jade set her new drink on the table.

"Izzy." Holden looked at Drew, then at Darby, then back at me and winked, which I knew was not flirting. I'd made a friend.

There was my opening. But I was not going to admit to strangers young enough to call me Aunt Izzy that my boyfriend, and just about everything they were praising me for, was fake.

Jade turned to me and shifted back her shoulder. She appeared even taller. "We're doing this. It's an important component for the growth of the brand. So, either it's you or someone else."

"I'm not forty yet. You want me to lie?" I said it before I could stop myself.

"Oh, that's just details! We need you to keep writing about your dates. You know, like the guy who picked his nose?"

Of course *he* was real.

I'd forgotten Jade and her team were the blogging CIA. I

thought of the screen names and avatars of my readers. Would they follow me to Pop Philly or would they feel abandoned? Hadn't I abandoned them already by disappearing for days without explanation? I knew that blogs ran cold, disappeared without notice, and that bloggers dissolved back into their real lives without any thought of their RSS feeds. But I also knew that for some people, these personal gigs came with online social responsibility and a little bit of blogger guilt. I wasn't sure where I fit in. I had just wanted to share stories, commiserate with others—not be the Pied Piper of the over-forty crowd, leading them out of the dregs of singlehood. If I could do it for others, I'd have done it for myself.

"You've got the chance to be a big voice for men and women who are terrified about having to date again. You can help people move past their exes. Or just move forward. I was going to offer you this gig before you needed it. It's kismet, honey. Blogging *beshert*! Totally meant to be! You can make some money—so you don't have to blast Bruce just yet, and you'll help me build my business."

"Why can't I blog about books or kids or parenting? I'm a counselor, I could really be a resource for your readers."

"Ho-hum, hon." Holden patted my hand. "Sorry. We're *Pop* Philly. Not *Snooze* Philly."

"We want the sincerity of Dear Abby with a splash of Kardashian." Jade flicked all her fingers in the air as if releasing confetti.

"We like a little glitz with our morning coffee, right?" Darby looked at Drew. "Don't worry, I'll help you get on the right track. Anything for the greater good."

"Thanks, Darb. I knew this would work!" Jade put her arm around my shoulders again. I shifted under its weight. "You'll give all the advice that's fit to print, so to speak. And you don't have to reveal your identity until you're ready. Guys, I'm going to talk to Izzy about the details. Drew? We'll talk later?"

He nodded.

"I recognize him." I whispered into Jade's ear. "Who *is* he?"

"I'll tell you later."

Then with a gentle tug, Jade led me away from the table to a crowded corner of the bar, which seemed to open like the Red Sea when Jade appeared. It was now or never. There was no Mac. The words stuck in my throat. I'm not even over Bruce. Well, not completely. The notions dizzied me. Courting lies and denial was a breeze compared to ramping up to tell the truth.

"You need a little more 'this' in your life." Jade pretended she was Vanna White and showcased the Chihuly-esque lighting, the tables full of animated people, and the whimsical food not meant for children. "I know you love being a guidance counselor. I know you have your own social life. But you need something that's just for you and just about you. And I can do that for you, Pea, if you do *this* for us. For me. I really need your help. I need to boost traffic. Please." Jade cocked her head the way she had done in the days when she wanted me to type her term papers. Then she scribbled onto a cocktail napkin, channeled her inner used-car salesman, and slid the napkin across the bar to me.

"This will be your monthly pay. Enough to pay for day care, right? Plus a little extra? Not only that, but doing this will take up enough space in your head to push out other things."

Jade was right. The amount was enough to cover Noah's before-and-after-school care, and maybe some of his speech-therapy sessions not covered by insurance. The rationalizations poured through me: I could blog about dating until Bruce got his act together. I'd still be anonymous, so no one would know it was written by me. Except Jade. And Rachel and Holden and Darby and Drew and the others at the table who remained nibbling, sipping blurs. But I could give advice and help people. It's what I did. I was a helper. It's not as if I didn't have common sense, even if I didn't always use it. I liked the idea of a little glitz with my coffee, and I needed to know I could do it. All of it.

I stared at the napkin and folded it into an origami disaster. Mrs. Feldman would not have been impressed.

"I can be anonymous, right?"

"You be whoever you want to be. Anyone with an understanding of reverse analytics and who has a half hour to kill could uncover any anonymous blogger, but they'd have to be looking. Really looking. Just use the Pop Philly interface and you'll be fine."

All I understood was "you'll be fine."

"This is not a pity job, Pea, this is a job-job. You're helping both of us. Remember that." How did she always read my mind except when I needed her to? "This is what bloggers dream about—recognition and money. I'm offering both, and I'm not asking you to give up your privacy. You deserve everything that's about to happen."

That's what I was afraid of.

— *Chapter* 5 —

Baby in the Air

A WEEK AFTER JADE offered me the Pop Philly job, and four days after Bruce left for California for his nonjob, I became a pirate.

"Walk the plank," Noah said, pointing at me as he bounded down the steps and walked bowlegged, hands on his hips, into the living room.

Noah had declared a moratorium on web slinging by shoving all his blue and red paraphernalia under his bed. I knew it was because Spider-Man made Noah think of his dad. One day, in grown-up, paid-for-by-his-own-health-insurance sessions, his therapist will tell him he wished it were Bruce he was shoving under the bed, or how removing the visual cues to his last time with Bruce made him store away those memories. I ached with Noah's underlying sadness. Bruce's departure was an addendum to our divorce, another way he left and didn't come back. At the moment, he was two for two.

Amateur psychoanalysis aside, it was much easier to be a pirate than Spider-Man. For starters, the costuming offered a little more leeway. I embraced it with a bandanna and a plastic eye patch held on, as Noah's was, with a giant rubber band. I duct-taped a Disney bird to the shoulder of Noah's sweatshirt. He giggled when he looked in the mirror and saw Zazu perched and secure. Then he darted into the kitchen, returning with two paper-towel tubes from the recycle bin. He handed one to me.

"Ha-yah!" Noah leapt into a fight stance, wielding his cardboard sword with contagious delight.

"Ha-yah!" The doorbell rang. "Avast, matey. Let me see who shot off that cannon."

It was Dreadlocks=Holden, with a backpack, a duffel bag, and Darby.

"Ahoy, matey," he said.

Darby smirked and closed one eye tight. My eye patch!

"These are friends of Auntie Jade's, Noah. We have some work to do, so you can watch TV." He looked at me wide-eyed, as if I never allowed him to watch TV.

Noah tore the parrot from his shoulder and galloped into the living room. He never walked. He ran or hopped, skipped or even ambled on all fours, but he never just walked. No matter where Noah was headed, he anticipated joy upon arrival.

Holden glided through the foyer and into the dining room, plopping his backpack on the table without a sound. I swiveled around to thank Darby for coming, but she had followed Noah into the living room.

"You'll be up and running in no time," Holden said.

"Huh? Oh, right." I watched Darby. She sat on the floor by Noah's feet. Her legs crossed at her ankles, her back against the sofa, she tipped back her head and talked. I couldn't hear a word, but she was interesting enough for Noah to move his eyes from the TV to the top of her head, or maybe to her eyes, or her nose ring. I couldn't tell. What did he think of the jewelry in Darby's nose? Pirates wore earrings. Noah would probably ask for one later.

"You're going to need to pay attention." Holden tapped my arm twice. "They're fine. Darby is *okay*."

"Oh, I know." Did I? "Sorry, I guess I don't understand why she's here if she's not working with us."

"She just wanted to come along, I hope that's all right." Holden emptied his backpack of a silver laptop, a jumble of wires, and a few small, black boxes. It looked to me as if he were going to build a robot. "Darbs said she'd never been to this neighborhood. Plus, we knew the little guy would be here. His dad left, right?"

I shuddered. Why was Holden asking such a personal question? That was out of line, none of his business, and frankly, embarrassing.

"Excuse me?"

"California. You said the little guy's dad went to California."

"I did?"

"You'd had a lot to drink."

What else had I said? "Yeah, he is in California. On business. He'll be back as soon as he can be, of course."

There I was again. Defending Bruce.

"Anyway, Darbs just thought that maybe he'd like some

company while you were busy. That's all." Holden tapped on his laptop, then mine, looking at one while he typed away on the other. "Where did you meet him, anyway?"

"Who?"

"Your boyfriend. Mac. The guy you're writing about. How'd you meet?"

Mac! "How did we *meet*?" Think, Izzy, think. Was it on JDate? "Uh, it's a long story."

"I'm updating the software on your laptop." He tapped my keyboard and looked at his watch, oversize and expensive looking. Probably from a street vendor, as were my Rolex, Coach, and Gucci everythings. "We have time."

"You know, now that I think of it, maybe it's better if I don't write about Mac, or dating at all."

Holden tapped and held a combination of keys. It looked as if he were playing the piano. He pushed the monitor toward me. "We've already designed the logo, see?"

Philly over Forty. I saw.

"And if you click on the bio . . ." A photo flanked by Internet gibberish jumped onto the screen. "The text goes in later. It'll be set up by tonight and ready to go for tomorrow."

"Who's that?" Red Phillies cap tipped down over a face, fingers clamped on the brim, partial jawline visible. Neck and shoulders visible, too. "Wait, is that supposed to be me?"

"It is you. And it's going up tonight with your bio."

"It's me?" I turned Holden's laptop toward me. I wanted to lift the cap and see the face. Instead, I just moved my face closer to the screen as if I could peek under it. "Are you sure?"

But I knew. Jade had snapped that picture at the Bank.

Citizens Bank Park. Bruce's boss had given him Diamond Club seats, and we took Jade and Lyle, her summer love that year, to the Phillies game. I was eight months pregnant, with blotchy skin, my long hair tucked in and through the half-moon above the adjustable strap. The sky was wake-up blue—bright enough to be a crayon in my box of sixty-four. For me, the color, the sky, meant the day was to be perfect, but I'd ended up dehydrated, with swollen ankles, and the designated driver. And the Phillies had lost.

"You don't want to show your face. No face. You're completely incognito."

I agreed, in theory. Unless you knew me, or what the side of my hand looked like, or had a personal memory of that day with me, you wouldn't recognize me. But I knew. I knew what was under the brim without looking at my face. It wasn't just the sky that was devoid of clouds that day. My life was also clear and bright. Bruce and I had discovered our newlywed mojo: we were expecting a baby, we'd bought our 1930s semidetached in Chestnut Hill, and we'd planted perennials. Nothing said forever like peonies and a DIY kitchen renovation.

"So, have you talked to Jade about the concept change? What is the new concept, anyway? I'm not sure I have time for a redesign before tomorrow." Holden scratched his head. "You know, they're really sure this is going to be the answer."

Who was they? And the answer to what?

I squinted, watching Holden as if I could memorize his actions, absorb his knowledge. His constant tapping ate into my brain. How. Am. I. Goingtodothis. What. The. Hellwas-Ithinking.

Holden pushed my laptop toward me as if he thought I couldn't see it was right there in front of me. But then I finally saw what he was showing me. A skillfully designed page with mock headlines and columns for text and advertising, all color-coordinated with the rest of Pop Philly. I was entranced, thinking of my *Bizzy Blog* with its free polka-dot template. *Philly over Forty* was sophisticated. Not too old. Not too young. Just right. Words and pictures rearranged every time he clicked to another page and then back to my own. Blank as a new canvas, where I'd be painting unicorns. My pulse quickened. This was big. Too big. This was Broadway, not dinner theater.

"I don't think I can do this."

"Sure you can. Or Jade wouldn't have asked you."

"Why is this so important to her?"

"It's the direction she wants to go with Pop Philly. And Drew's all for it. So that definitely helps. We need something unique—something special—to help us bring in more advertisers."

"I thought the Web site was doing really well."

"There's a lot of competition. We always need more traffic to attract more big advertisers. People like Drew."

There was Coat Guy again.

"Jade can explain. She's the brain and the face behind the site. But I don't have to tell *you* about Jade."

Maybe he did.

"I'm setting you up with our software, and hooking you into our network."

Forty minutes and seven pages of shorthand notes later, I was logged in behind the scenes.

"I'm not sure I can do this."

"Of course you can."

Holden was very wrong.

"What will happen if I don't?"

"Nothing."

Silence followed. Then Holden smiled. "C'mon, you'll be fine. This part is like a closet where you hide all your junk before company comes over."

If only he knew.

"You really enjoy this, don't you?"

"Yeah. How'd you know?" He didn't look at me, but he smiled.

"It's my job to notice things. I like figuring out people and what they need to do to get what they want." I'd helped hundreds of students over the past fifteen years. Holden could even have been one of them.

"What do I need?" He crossed his arms over his chest and leaned back in the chair. He wasn't challenging me, he was asking me.

"Right now you need to find a way to convince me not to back out."

Holden laughed. "What do *you* need?"

It was the question of the day. Month. Year. Lifetime. I shrugged like one of my students.

"Then how do you know *this* isn't it?"

I didn't, but doubt crept into my psyche. Plus, trying to say no to Holden was like trying to say no to a two-year-old who handed me a toy phone and said, "Answer it."

Holden pulled out his real phone. "I can text the team and tell them to pull the page."

"No, don't. I'll do it."

Just then, Darby walked into the room with Noah.

"Hey, kiddo," I said. "Having fun?"

Noah looked up at Darby and nodded. She rustled his hair and smiled. For that moment, my misgivings subsided.

"Noah says you haven't lived here very long," she said.

Because five-year-olds are great arbiters of time. "Technically, he's right. But I grew up in this house."

"So now you've come home to roost. The neighborhood is so cute."

I turned away before I smacked her.

"So, you're all set?" Darby didn't wait for an answer; she just leaned over and tapped on my laptop. "Looks great. I can't wait to see what you come up with."

"Excuse me?"

"I can't wait to find out more about Mac."

Me, too.

"It's all a little strange, wouldn't you say?" Darby added.

"What do you mean?" She couldn't mean . . .

"Darb, stop," Holden said.

"I have a following on Pop Philly, but Jade brings in not only an *unknown*—but someone who wants to be anonymous."

Holden stood. "You know we need ad revenue. And you know Jade was looking for something new and different. Cut it out."

"Fine. Just—it must be nice to have your best friend for a boss and a great gig."

She didn't say *one you don't deserve,* but I heard it anyway.

"What's a gig? Can I have one?" All of a sudden Noah was paying attention to what the grown-ups were saying. Again.

I opened my eyes wide at Holden.

"Hey, buddy, I'm thirsty. Would you walk me to the kitchen to get a glass of water?"

One point for Holden. Okay, ten points. I shifted my attention to Darby, who was racking up the demerits.

"I don't discuss my social life, or my blogging, with Noah," I whispered. "So I'd appreciate it if you didn't either."

Darby zipped her lips and threw away the key.

— Chapter 6 —

Freeze Tag

Mrs. Feldman said Mac was my secret, but I'd never thought of him as that. My stash of chocolate-covered espresso beans behind the oatmeal in my pantry—that was a secret. Being accepted to law school—a secret. Doubling up on Spanx under my Rosh Hashanah suit—a secret.

Mac wasn't a secret at all. He was a *lie*. Secrets belonged to their keepers. Lies belonged to everyone. I'd enlisted innocent bystanders in my ruse, elicited emotions, garnered interaction. Secrets were kept. Lies were shared. When I wrote about my first real date, comments soared. And the date had been awful! Then I wrote about another date. I didn't know why, but I embellished a bit with descriptions and dialogue, used my imagination, added a little flair. Then I did it again. The worse the date, the higher the hits. I was a living social experiment gone awry. Then I wrote about the sweatshirt twins, and about telling Bruce ("The Ex") and Amber ("The Girlfriend") about my having a boyfriend. The next day the comments had surged. I should have known that all single parents dealt with raging feelings of inadequacy—whether they acknowledged them or not. The post had been pinged and linked and forwarded all over the Internet. Comments and e-mails poured in from women who were thinking about divorce, women who were divorced, and even from a few men. I was lauded for my bravery and chided for my cowardice, all with a few taps of the touch pad. It had become too real too fast. And now the lie was on steroids.

Welcome to *Philly over Forty*, your one-stop shop for all things dating-over-forty. I'm your host—the one in the cap, the one you can't really see. That's because I work with kids, have a kid of my own, and an ex-husband of my own to boot. You don't have to be a single parent to get what that means. It means there's a line that I won't cross. But that doesn't mean I won't share. I will. I'll share my dating experiences. (Like the guy who asked me to pay for my croissant because "the date was for coffee.") I'll share my notes on the best places to go. (Good Dog Bar's happy-hour vibe is reassuring for the nervous dater.) And the worst. (I've never been to Wedge+Fig when at least one couple wasn't celebrating an anniversary.) Mostly, though, I'll share the madness, the angst, and that euphoria that accompanies dating over forty in our city and beyond.

Dating is hard. But you don't have to go it alone.

I blinked. I blinked again. This might actually work. I might actually be able to pull this off. But that was just the intro. How was I going to write about a weekend date I didn't go on with a boyfriend I didn't have? Had I misjudged my capacity to lie? And why on earth would that be a bad thing?

I may not have had an idea for a blog post, but I did have ideas about Noah. We were together in the house, breathing the same air, yet—stellar mother that I was—I had plugged Noah into a movie in my bedroom along with a peanut butter sandwich, sliced apples, and a snack-size Milky Way. A bed-top picnic instead of a playdate. I had ignored the lure of the snow, the tug of the sky, the compulsion to be together instead of apart. I might as well have been in California with Bruce and Amber, or have been my mother, who spent most evenings of my childhood lounging on our sofa, wearing a housecoat. My dad would be doing paperwork. I never knew what that was. My parents had been close at hand but far away. I sat on *my* sofa and stared at my lap. And my yoga pants. Oh no. Yoga pants were the new housecoats.

"Noah? Want to play outside with Mommy?" I yelled as I walked to the foot of the staircase. He still coveted our time together. I knew I always would.

I yelled it again. Nothing. Those yellow minions had latched onto his brain and stolen his attention. Or more likely, they'd allowed him to forget that he hadn't talked to Bruce the night before. Still, I couldn't believe that the promise of a snowball fight and snow angels would go unheeded.

I was halfway up the stairs when Noah appeared before me wearing so many layers of clothing he looked like the Stay Puft Marshmallow Man.

He'd heard me loud and clear.

I was sure our block was the last to be plowed, but I liked the way the snow made the street bright as day at night, and how it covered the sidewalk's imperfections always. The cement had so many cracks that as a child I wondered if there weren't broken mothers' backs all over our neighborhood.

I still labeled each house on Good Street with its long-ago residents' names. The house right across the street was the Mason house. I looked toward the Baker, Elliot, and DiNardo houses, then toward the Roberts, Maxwell, and Perry houses at the far end of the street. All those kids were grown, like me, and the families had long ago left for the shore, the suburbs, or Florida. But their ghostly presence warmed me. If I stared long enough at any front door and closed my one eye (with one eye on Noah), I could see my friends at various ages as if they'd never left. I could hear their parents calling them in for dinner through screen doors and out of windows. But they hadn't stayed like Mrs. Feldman, or come back, like me. We were the old-timers, the resident minders of memories.

"Uncle Ethan and Uncle Eddie built an igloo one year for me." Having older brothers had been wonderful. Sometimes.

"What's an igloo?"

A cooler that holds beer. "Where Eskimos live." Now I was perpetuating ethnic stereotypes.

"Where do pirates live?" Noah's speech was still speckled with tricky *r*'s. "Where do pirates live?" He said it extra slow so that I would both hear and understand.

"Probably on their ships."

"Then I better build some beds."

Noah smiled at me and crinkled his runny nose. I held

out a tissue and he waddled over; I wiped, then joined in the building.

Soon we were surrounded by new friends—none other than Snow Captain Hook and Snow Mr. Smee, who donned eye patches, bandannas, and even a plastic hook stuck into the spot usually reserved for an arm branch. Our patio became the ship, the same way it had been the house or the school or the restaurant when I was growing up. We had a real American flag and a brown cardboard plank, and the ship's steering wheel was an aluminum-foil pizza pan. We stood our broom mast in the corner against the railing, near the beds that we'd made out of lawn chairs.

Noah's lips were still pink when I checked beneath his scarf. We had time to finish our pirate scene before we turned to pillars of ice.

I watched my boy, his deliberate movements packing snow in small handfuls into divots on the side of Snow Smee. Then Noah stepped back, far enough to see the pirates, the ship, the plank, the flag. He smiled so wide his eyes closed. Perhaps he was just imprinting the memory, too special to let go. I closed my eyes as well.

Like a little old lady who pulls up her chair to the edge of the water at the beach, just waiting for the edges of a spent wave to wash over her feet, I sat and waited for Noah to finish with his boy touches. An extra-big nose for Snow Hook and some muscles. I wiggled my toes and willed them to warm, as my thoughts filtered back to me and Mac. He was the kind of guy who'd build snowmen. Or he would be if he existed. I could make that part of our magical imaginary weekend. I'd make it fabulous. That would be fun to write. Although as Noah threw his wet, frozen arms around my neck, I knew nothing could be better than what I was doing right now.

A white Mercedes sedan drove up the street and stopped in front of my house. Mrs. Feldman's house. Same place. Then her front door opened. I hadn't even thought to invite her to sit with me in the snow, to direct snow-pirate and snow-ship building. Would she have liked that? Sitting in the snow wasn't something my mother would have done. But then, my mother was not Mrs. Feldman. She emerged bundled in faux-fur-topped boots and a long quilted coat. Was this another of her ladies' days out? A book club? A movie? She had a better social life than I did.

"You've been busy," she said, grasping the metal railing.

I rose to help her down our shared steps. In the middle of the street, someone emerged from the driver's side of the car.

"You okay, Ma?"

"Ray, I'm fine." The Feldman boys were older than my brothers, so I knew them only as visitors as I was growing up. But I did look at family photos as I dusted the frames on occasion. The photos had given me some insight into their lives; I made up the rest. I was good at that.

The passenger door opened and Ray's wife, Meredith, stepped out. She walked to the sidewalk without glancing back toward her husband.

Mrs. Feldman held my arm tight as we descended the steps.

"We have twelve-thirty reservations."

Ray said it loud and Meredith shook her head. Show-off. Just like in the photos where he flexed his muscles or held up trophies. Mrs. Feldman looked at me and whispered loud enough for Ray to hear, "Because if I don't eat a fancy brunch, I will starve."

Was it a special occasion and I'd forgotten? Mrs. Feldman's birthday was near mine, in March. I knew she'd be eighty-six, but the end of January seemed early for a celebration. And Ray didn't seem the type to splurge on a random Sunday.

He looked away, avoiding my laser-beam glance. I walked Mrs. Feldman to Meredith, not letting go until the two women linked arms. And like a parent giving away a bride, I prayed she was in loving hands.

"You look pretty, Ma," Ray said.

Meredith walked Mrs. Feldman to the car, and Ray came around and opened the door to the backseat.

"Have a nice time today, Mrs. Feldman!"

She turned to me and shook her head. Mrs. Feldman wanted me to call her Geraldine.

But there was just something about *Mrs. Feldman.*

— Chapter 7 —

Mousetrap

WITH MY MATERNAL WELL filled, my limbs thawed, and Noah playing Angry Birds on my laptop, I felt a lightening, an ease of tension in my shoulders. Then I checked my phone. Six texts and two missed voice mails from Jade.

"Where have you been?"

"Outside playing with Noah."

"In this weather?"

"It was fun."

"Okay, okay, I'll take your word for it. Do you have a little time now?"

Jade respected the responsibilities of parenting, I knew that. She built blanket forts that put Boy Scouts to shame, read more books aloud than a librarian on NoDoz. She knew the value of the latest toy and the value of a roll-around snuggle on the floor. But she didn't pretend to understand the unfettered joy of motherhood or the pangs of parenting guilt. She didn't want to.

"I'm here now," I said as I side-hopped onto the kitchen

counter. It was my go-to spot for talking on the phone since the days when the cord only reached that far. "What's on fire?"

"I wanted to explain more about what's going on with *P-O-F*."

"P-O-F?"

"Philly over Forty?"

Jade loved acronyms as much as she hated air quotes.

I wished for a phone cord to twist away my nerves. "Tell me everything I need to know."

"I needed an influx of cash for Pop Philly and Drew provided it."

"The guy from Meema's? Why?" Coat Guy was a cash cow?

"Because we're friends. I met him years ago and just gave him a call. I thought it would be a good fit, and it was—or it will be."

"I'm not taking your money if things are this bad."

"They're not awful. Not yet. It's just taking a lot more money than I thought it would to upgrade and hire really good people. Drew's money buys him ad space, and the cash helps me. It's a win-win. Plus, he has a lot of good ideas, so he's like an unofficial adviser."

Jade talked faster than I could think. I let my thoughts catch up to her words. I knew the site had ads, but I hadn't given much thought as to how Pop Philly paid for itself, for Jade, for me. For anything.

"So, these ads . . ." I said.

"Are going to sponsor *P-O-F*."

Coat Guy was my sugar daddy.

"The more people who see the ads, the more valuable you and Pop Philly are to Drew and to other potential advertisers. So, you need to engage your readers. Let them get to know you, to get inside your life."

I felt the pounding of love for my friend. I felt contempt for myself.

"I just want to write the blog posts, J." I shimmied off the counter and walked around in a circle. "I thought you said I got to do this on my own time and post three times a week. That's not a big commitment."

"Things have changed a bit, but you'll be fine, I promise."

"What things have changed?"

"I hoped this would be big, Pea, but I didn't realize how big it could be, and Drew agrees. Launching this new section of Pop Philly gives us a whole new reach. It's not just about dating and it's not just about you and Mac. It's about the city from a new angle. It's exciting, it's going to open doors. You should be excited! Today's weekend traffic has been a third higher than usual. There are singles in their forties who are parents, and some who aren't parents. Some are divorced, some never married. What do they all have in common? They all want to know how to navigate the wild frontier of dating over forty. And you're going to show them!" Jade stopped talking. "You didn't realize how many people were going to see this, did you? Or how important it was?"

"I know how big Pop Philly is, Jade." I didn't know, but I knew. I knew that Jade was listed as one of *Philly* magazine's most eligible entrepreneurs under forty, and as one of B'nai B'rith's Forty Under Forty. And I knew that the teachers and staff at Liberty were smitten with Pop Philly as soon as I mentioned—okay, *bragged*—that my best friend started it. "But this is not what I signed up for. This is not what we talked about." How much had we both had to drink that night at Meema's? "I thought I was supposed to write about my dates and being a single mom who's dating. Maybe parcel out bits of advice. Maybe a recipe or two. And be anonymous. Don't forget anonymous."

"Anonymous doesn't cancel out popular. Some of the most popular bloggers out there started out anonymous, or with a pseudonym. And it didn't start with blogging. Think about Dear Abby!"

"I'm not just starting out anonymous. I'm staying anonymous."

"Fine. I need to keep Drew happy. Because the stakes just got higher."

"For who?"

"For everyone! I hope you're taking this seriously because it's going to be seriously big."

"Well, talking about big, I was thinking of sort of changing the focus of the blog a little bit. I mean, I saw the logo and that photo of me you dug up, but—"

"Impossible."

"What do you mean, impossible?"

"I promised an always-introspective, sometimes hot, look into the world of dating in our forties—and he committed to thousands of dollars' worth of ads for the next three months. So, yes, impossible."

"Hot? I'm supposed to write *hot*?"

"Hey, if your dates with Mac aren't hot, that's not my fault. Drew knows that."

My insides rippled. I said nothing.

"It was a joke, Pea. Oh my God, are you okay? Did something happen with Mac? If it did, don't tell me. Just find a new guy really fast." She chuckled.

Maybe I'll name this one Dell.

"Is this friend Jade or boss Jade?" Apparently there was a difference.

"It's just me. What happened? Do you still want to do this? Let me know if I need to dial 1-888-LAWMANN." She sang the jingle that went along with tacky TV commercials.

"What does Andrew Mann have to do with this?" He was "the Delaware Valley's number one divorce lawyer," with billboards on I-95 to prove it.

"What do you mean, what does he have to do with it? I just explained it to you."

"*Drew* is Andrew Mann?" Now I knew why he looked familiar.

"I thought you knew."

"If I had, I wouldn't have let him hold my coat."

Mrs. Feldman was coming for Sunday dinner. My version of Sunday dinner. Pizza. I'd invited her before, but she'd always declined. You'd think she needed to ride the bus, get a transfer, hop on the el, and then walk six blocks. But, since I'd moved back, we always seemed to talk at her house. I was thrilled she'd agreed to come over. I shuddered with giddiness and flitted around as if expecting a date, not my next-door neighbor.

We all used the smallest-size paper-towel squares and patted away the grease atop our pizza slices. My phone vibrated in my pocket and I ignored it. When it didn't beep to indicate a message had been left, I knew it wasn't important. It could have been Bruce, but I wasn't going to ruin our pizza party. Not yet.

We folded the slices in half and each took a bite. Grease funneled out of Noah's slice; I took it from him and dried the top.

"I think that's supposed to be there. Or they wouldn't put it there." His speech was clearer sometimes, more confident. The improvements were intermittent, yet present.

"If you wipe it away, you'll have room for dessert," Mrs. Feldman said.

Noah took the paper towel and dabbed until the glistening cheese had a matte finish. And lint.

I allowed Noah to take the pizza into the living room and sit on my dad's recliner with a tray on his lap. It was nice to have a relaxing Sunday dinner after a busy day, and what would be a busy night. I slid another piece of pizza onto my plate. "Thank you for coming over here tonight. Noah and I had a busy day, and I know he likes just being able to hang out here. Not that he's not comfortable at your house, he is. And I am."

"You don't have to explain. There's no place like home."

She winked at me. Sharp as a tack, that one. Her cliché tendencies were rubbing off on me and I didn't mind.

"What's it like being home, Elizabeth? Living in the house where you were a little girl?"

"I can't really compare it to anything. It just *is*." Until now I had pushed aside the shame of moving back home and replaced it with optimism. "It was either move here or find an apartment somewhere unfamiliar. The elementary school is still good, but I thought . . ." My thoughts wandered out the window and onto the empty sidewalk. "I thought it would be more like it was when I grew up—with lots of kids for Noah to play with. With neighbors sitting outside on the steps at night—I mean, not now, but in the fall. I didn't realize then how abandoned it would seem. I was too busy moving in and getting the new carpet, painting, figuring out how it would all work. It's not that I don't like being here. It's so familiar, I guess. I don't think about it." I kept putting my foot right into my mouth along with the pizza. "I do think about you. I'm glad you're here. That makes up for a lot."

"I think you're brave. Going back can sometimes feel like going backwards. But you seem to be moving forward somewhat. I'm not sure I could've done that."

"Done what?" We cleared the table and threw away the paper plates. I kept my back to her, knowing she didn't like to answer questions about herself. I kept moving around the kitchen, wiping the counter, pretending I wasn't interested that much. Maybe she'd keep talking.

"Girls in my day didn't do all the things you girls do now."

I turned around. Mrs. Feldman had never before expressed an ounce of serious discontent. "What did you want to do that you didn't get to do?"

"I would have liked to have gone to college, but my parents

said there was no reason for a girl to go. I lived at home with them until I married Sol."

"How old were you when you got married?"

"Twenty-three. My parents thought I was going to be a spinster."

I laughed, but Mrs. Feldman wasn't laughing. Then she shook away her staid demeanor and smiled. "I knew Sol from shul. He was older than me and he led the junior congregation services when I was growing up. Then he went away to war, like all the boys did. We met him again years later. I'd always thought he was handsome and had wanted to sit in the front row and just stare at him as he davened. Who knew praying could be so sexy?" She blushed. "But it was. My parents said he was a nice boy. A boy! He was twenty-eight. I think deep down we both thought it was our last chance. So we got married."

"Just like that?"

"Just like that."

"And since we were both already living in the neighborhood, it was easy to move next door. No stress of going somewhere new."

"I knew you grew up around here, but Mr. Feldman did, too?"

"Yes, right over on Beecham Street."

"Do you wish you'd just gotten married and moved away?"

"Where would we go? Plus, I couldn't think of living anywhere else but Good Street."

"Why not?"

"My parents moved to Good Street when I was fifteen."

"You lived on Good Street when you were growing up?"

"Yes. In this house."

"*This* house?" How did I not know this? Why had she never told me?

"Yes." Mrs. Feldman leaned back in her chair and against the wall, as if settling in for story time. "My parents sold this house to your parents. But when Sol and I got married years before that, we moved in right next door. My parents wanted me close. I wanted to be close, I didn't know any different. It's what families did back then. Two of my aunts moved around the corner, so my cousins were here, too. Which was easier when I started a new high school when I was sixteen."

"You lived in *my* house!"

"No, you grew up in *my* house!"

We laughed and the invisible thread between us tugged. Our lives had been sewn together long before I sat in Mrs. Feldman's kitchen after school, long before she was my teenage confidant, my surrogate mother-grandmother-friend. We were not connected by blood but by bricks. Sturdy, impenetrable, permanent bricks.

"Why didn't you tell me? This is something I could have known since I was little."

"It didn't seem important. I'd moved on. Different house, different life."

"Not important?"

"I was fifteen when we moved here. And believe me, I was fully grown."

"Do you want to walk around? Go into the bedrooms? The

basement . . ." She hadn't been in this house for seven months. Or was it seven years? I had few memories of Mrs. Feldman in my house. Ever.

"No. But I know what I do want to do."

"What? Anything."

"I want to make good on that promise of dessert for Noah."

I'd eaten two cupcakes before I had the nerve to mention Mrs. Feldman's brunch with Ray and Meredith. "Was it a special occasion?"

"No, but it was too fancy."

I couldn't very well ask about Ray's motives for taking his mother to a five-star brunch. "I bet it was nice to spend time with them."

"It would have been if the other boys hadn't called on Ray's cell phone while we were there. They ambushed me."

Manny, Moe, and Jack, my father had called them, as if he couldn't remember their names. For short he just referred to them as the Pep Boys. And that's how I thought of them, standing solid atop their store on the Boulevard, but without any pep.

"Why would they do that to you?"

Mrs. Feldman flinched, surprised by my push. Usually I allowed her words to float between us without consequence.

"They wanted to talk to me about financial matters. My will. My bank accounts. My bookkeeping. Wanted to know how all my paperwork is organized. Which of course it is. You know I'm still the treasurer of the synagogue Sisterhood. And every penny is accounted for."

I did know.

"I promised them it's all divided equally when I'm gone. But that's not enough, they want to see it all for themselves. I'm almost eighty-six, but that doesn't automatically mean I'm losing my marbles."

I saddened at the thought, but eighty-five *was* eighty-five. Would this be one of those stories where a modest, kindly old woman dies and leaves millions to her cat? No cat. And from what I could tell, no millions either. It seemed reasonable that her sons wanted to see her will. They wanted to take care of her, make sure her affairs were in order. But what could they be after? Her Lladró collection, kitschy keepsakes, a few pieces of real jewelry?

I'd just want one of her napkins, already folded.

I walked to the living room to check on Noah and to change the course of my thoughts. Mrs. Feldman had always been next door. Even when I wasn't. I couldn't think of her living anywhere else, let alone anything worse.

Chapter 8

Miss Mary Mack

My best ideas came when least expected—somewhat like colds and old boyfriends—so I postponed writing my next blog post. I logged on to Facebook instead, knowing that I'd lose myself in the grown-up faces of my childhood friends and the doppelgängers they showcased as their offspring. I answered a few quizzes that quantified my life. My accent was from Philadelphia. I most resembled the literary heroine Jane Eyre. I should live in Paris. I was 90 percent a foodie. I stopped before finding out who I'd been in a previous life. One life was enough for now, thank you very much.

I had nothing on my own Facebook page except a profile picture from an excellent hair day and a bevy of last year's birthday wishes. The last comment on Rachel's page had been entered three minutes before.

I tried not to notice the photo that flanked Rachel's name at the top of her page. Head tilted, eyes looking up, hair full and pushed to one side. Like a glamour shot without the painted lips or feather boa. I cast down my gaze, embarrassed on Rachel's behalf. Who was this Real Housewife of Rydal, and what had she done with my herb-growing, ballet-loving cousin?

I looked through Rachel's photos. Arielle and Miriam dressed as Queen Esthers for Purim. Levi and Jacob lighting Hanukkah candles with Noah, all with yarmulkes askew. Photos of Thanksgiving at her mother's house. Photos of Rachel and her friends, Rachel and the kids, the kids on their own. I recognized the back of my head by my long-lost ponytail. But where was Seth? I found one family photo, posed, in front of a white background, taken at Fun Time Photo at the mall, everyone dressed in jeans and white shirts, no shoes or socks. A classic that somehow felt outdated.

I looked away from the screen, disoriented, a little like Mr. Magoo in "Rip Van Winkle," which I had watched with my brothers. I glanced at the corner of the monitor. Nine thirty. I'd been bouncing around online for an hour and a half in search of inspiration. All I had now was the bad feeling that accompanies procrastination and the knowledge that time spent online traveled fast. I may not have gotten any work done, but at least I knew what all my high school friends had for breakfast.

I wondered what Mac might eat for breakfast. I didn't have to wonder. I just decided. Steel-cut oats. Mac was a healthy eater. That was a start.

I sat and typed, cup of tea by my side, Felix at my feet. This shouldn't be so hard. But it was. I'd been blogging for months and I had always enjoyed it. I was never at a loss as to what to write. But now that Jade was counting on me to help her—finally it was my turn to help her—I was all stopped up, as my mother would say.

I clicked to the front page of Pop Philly, the one I'd been avoiding because once I saw it, I knew it would be real. And there I was. On display and incognito. My Phillies cap stared at me as if it had eyes—other than the ones hidden beneath it. I loved that cap. I loved that newlywed mom-to-be and the hope that came with every kernel of popcorn and every sip of Coke. That Izzy Lane was the avatar for the eternal optimist. That Izzy Lane had not deleted her dreams. Her sense of adventure was real and true.

I needed that Izzy Lane right now.

I needed that cap.

Unfinished and cold, my basement was a constant reminder of the way my parents had spent my childhood. The owners of a hardware store that sold tools, paint, lumber, and even rolls of linoleum flooring did not have a finished basement.

I flipped on the light and left the door open, still convinced something untoward lived beneath the stairs.

The cap was somewhere among the cardboard boxes and Rubbermaid totes (labeled and not) my parents had left behind. It was easy to identify the boxes that I'd packed up when Bruce and I had split, the ones with the marriage mementos I thought might one day be meaningful to Noah. I zeroed in on four boxes labeled CHESTNUT HILL. Eeny, meeny, miny, moe. I tugged at meeny, not moe, something that always got me into trouble in games at school. I half expected to be greeted by Malibu Barbie or Mod Hair Ken, but I unfolded the top and on borrowed luck a red brim stuck out at me like a hand stretched out to help.

With the Phillies cap on my head, I walked around the living room. I felt silly. What was this? Method blogging? Did I think I'd become the younger me who didn't know about being left by a husband and leaving a dream house and encouraging her parents to leave their home so she could move in?

I needed reinforcements.

I texted Jade, afraid if we talked she would hear the fragility in my voice.

The intro post was easy. What should I write for my next one?

> You haven't written it yet? It goes live at 6 am.

Don't worry. Any ideas?

> Start with how you met Mac, how you juggle work and parenting and dating and add in some fun things to do on dates so there's some real reader takeaway. It's about you, but it's about the reader.

You've been thinking about this.

> That's my job. No, it's your job. Get busy, Pea. xo Pea?

Yes?

> Start at the beginning.

The beginning was the problem. I'd only been on a few dates in the past six months. Wrinkled-trench-coat guy who liked to hunt and fish and camp. Oh, deer! Dermatologist with acne scars who'd never love anyone but his first wife. Or his second. Handsome social worker who didn't drive and never called again even though I bought a fiberglass bike helmet and cooked him quinoa for dinner. *Philly over Forty* was supposed to be hip and hot. I chuckled. I had not gotten the hip-and-hot memo, nor had any of my dates. Maybe if I had read Pop Philly I'd have known what was popular, elusive, on the cusp of elegant, awesome, and fun.

Because fun for me? Saturday night in Target without Noah. Pushing the cart without someone riding on the end of it. Buying a one-gallon skim mocha latte and lamp-heated popcorn and skipping the red cart up and down every aisle with the abandon of a girl with a gift card.

Something told me that wasn't what Jade, the readers, or Andrew Mann wanted.

I had to get organized. It was part of my real job to be organized, keeping files on the students, for the different teachers, for the district, for myself. This was just keeping make-believe files.

One file for everything Mac and I had done and were planning to do. One file for how Mac looked and talked. Another for sweet things he said and my replies. Then I'd need another file to keep ideas for future dates, to make sure that if there was a repeat, it was because it was "ours." The pages filled. Mac was reliable, trustworthy, funny, and fun. He was handsome and tall. Jewish. He wasn't afraid of commitment. He was professional and dedicated to his work, but not a workaholic. He was a dentist; he rarely traveled for his job.

Is that what these people want to know? What would I want if I were at home reading *Philly over Forty,* looking for the perfect date night, funny story, or bit of advice?

God help me. I *was* them. I was the single mom who wanted to go out, do things, find someone, start over—even if my online persona said I'd already done it all. In real life I'd like a place to share my own stories—the crazy ones, the mundane ones, the ones no one wanted to listen to. The ones I didn't want to tell, but needed to tell. Then I realized what I had at my fingertips. It was more than storytelling. It was a place for single parents to share their tales of woe. *And whoa.* I had a place where they could share ideas that perhaps their friends and family didn't need or couldn't relate to. I'd still have to come up with something. I'd still have to make it seem real. I'd write about Mac. But only to set the stage to feature the readers, not me.

Where do you go when you're on your own for a weekend?

Best cheap restaurants for single parents and kids?

What was your worst date ever?

Tell us about your next first love.

How did you tell your kids about your divorce?

Do you go to restaurants by yourself? Which ones?

The questions flowed onto three pages.

I was going to get much more out of this gig than a paycheck.

And then—I knew. I knew even more about Mac and me. I knew all about our weekend. I closed my eyes and saw sails from visiting tall ships waving against an indigo sky, all in the foreground of the Ben Franklin Bridge. The scent of a pretzel cart, with the tang of Gulden's as the finish. Unlikely snapshots appropriate for fiction. Yet it seemed so real, as if I'd been there before or could be there again.

Reel it in, Izzy Rowling.

Then, a visceral memory—the pressure and warmth of holding a hand bigger than mine. It spread from my wrist to my fingertips, squeezing my hand closed, then my throat.

I wiped it from both, and typed.

Chapter 9

Double Dutch

My eyes fluttered open as if I'd had enough sleep, but my head faced away from my clock. What a treat to wake up on my own with unintended time to spare. I stretched and groaned the way I couldn't when I was busy slapping the top of the alarm clock to get nine more minutes.

It must have been about five forty-five. I'd savor those fifteen minutes. I rolled my neck and glanced at the clock. Maybe I even had twenty.

Damn.

It was six-thirty. Six-thirty! How could it be six-thirty? I didn't need to touch the clock to know. The clock didn't fail me, I had failed myself. The alarm button was set to OFF. I had never forgotten to set the alarm after a weekend. Until today.

Up and out of bed, I turned on the water for my shower, ran downstairs, plugged in the electric teakettle, and headed back upstairs. I'd lost a half hour. Up at six meant shower, Earl Grey, and the *Inquirer* (still the paper version), before I dressed and woke my boy at seven. Up at six meant time to myself to fill my lungs with the oxygen that would carry me through the day. Up at six meant I hadn't been up until two-thirty writing a blog post about my imaginary boyfriend and reading a thousand welcome messages to the imaginary me.

The same me who had to pack real lunches.

I had stayed up too late writing about Mac, deleting, and then writing again. I had more ideas and kept going. I wrote about Date Outfits: *Cover Up, Buttercup.* I wrote the interminable Should a Woman Split the Check on Date Number One: *No, Hon, the Time to Pay Is Not Today.* I wrote about Meeting a Date's Children Too Soon: *I Kid You Not, Don't Do It.* Then there was the Three-Date Rule: *Rules Are Meant to Be Broken (However You See Fit).* My words knocked into each other like dominoes. I hadn't stopped until I couldn't see the screen.

I'd woven intricate stories mixed with solid truths from my life that, in my mind, neutralized the lies. I was a divorced mom with a son in elementary school. I worked a full-time job. I had friends, a family, a few dates, a lot of opinions. The details of my posts were vibrant, but their true meaning, muted.

I drank my tea and read the paper as I blew dry my hair. It didn't matter I'd slept through my post going live on Pop Philly, or that I might have more comments on my intro. I didn't have the time to turn on my computer and investigate. I had a real day ahead of me with real students with real problems. And I had a real five-year-old who'd be awake in five minutes.

I pulled clothes out of the closet and looked at my clock, that digital Benedict Arnold. Had anyone read my post yet? Recognized my photo? Was I being heckled? No, Jade would have called if it were a disaster. She called me whenever she wanted.

Always had. I could just look, just for a minute. I could set an alarm so I woke up Noah in three minutes, and—no!

Life was going to backfire if I couldn't make all the pieces fit.

I'd drop Noah off a little late. I'd be a little later. I hadn't been late to work without a snowstorm to blame in over fifteen years.

Downstairs, I laid my hand atop the cool and silent laptop, as if to bless it. I could have sworn it jeered.

I opened my door just wide enough to poke my head out. Students leaned again the walls and sat on the blue plastic chairs lined up in the counseling office. The mix of sweat and coffee and air freshener tickled my nose even after fifteen years.

"Donna?"

Our department secretary turned from her desk in the middle of the wide-open space; waist-high walls surrounded her cubicle, as if a playpen for her workday. I walked over to Donna's station—much more than a secretary's desk—and looked at the sign-up sheet for student appointments. I didn't have an appointment until nine. I took a Flair pen from Donna's cup and put an *X* through the next half hour. I looked to my left and then my right, only willing to involve my colleague if she was out of earshot. The district had laid off two of our four counselors in the past two years. The pair of us with seniority had to cover each other not just sometimes, but all times. "If one of my students comes in, ask him to wait or ask Helen to cover." I'd make it up to her with a latte.

"Okay, Miss Lane. Are you all right?" She meant because I'd

scooted in ten minutes before, pretending I'd been in another part of the building.

"Yes, I'm fine. I just need a few minutes without interruptions."

"No problem, Miss Lane."

Donna wouldn't call me Izzy, even though I called her by her first name. She felt it sounded too "familiar," even after all this time working together every day. At the very least I wish she'd use *Ms.* instead of *Miss.* I guess I should be happy she didn't refer to me as *Mrs.* I shut my door and smiled at the image Donna projected—an urban, contemporary secretary, a throwback from the sixties, except she was a computer whiz. She sported a daily updo, pencil behind her ear even though she never wrote with a pencil, and knockoff wardrobe that didn't look it. She was older than me, but we'd never discussed by how much. Donna loved her job as our counseling-department secretary, a job she'd had before I joined the staff in 1999. I knew she was taking one class at night at Community College of Philadelphia and had been doing that for years. She had her sights set on a Temple degree in business. Donna moved slow and steady, holding tight to the handle of her dreams.

Safe behind a door that couldn't lock, I called Jade. I whispered even though no one could hear. "How's it going so far?"

"You didn't check?"

"J, I can't. You know my mornings are crazy. I have a lot going on. I didn't have time." I omitted the part about oversleeping. I didn't want Jade to think I couldn't handle Noah, Liberty, *Philly over Forty,* and life in general.

"We had four thousand views before eight. It's been shared a few hundred times. I love what you did! Writing about the first date you ever went on after you and Bruce split? Perfect!"

I smiled despite myself. That part of the post was true. How I dressed for my first date as a single mom while Noah was at Chuck E. Cheese with Bruce. As much as I loved hands-on parenting, winning tickets for cheap trinkets, and being stalked by a giant mouse, I couldn't help feeling triumphant. That weekend I was going to be the gal-about-town doing something that didn't include crayons or fluorescent lighting. Or that's what I'd thought, until my date showed up wearing a tucked-in Eagles jersey and suggested we go to Nifty Fifty's. That night, I deflated. Last night, I laughed.

"But why didn't you tell me you went to Lucy's *a couple of weeks ago*?" Jade asked. "I was right around the corner having a drink with Drew. We could have met you!"

Jade was having a drink with Andrew Mann? "Are you dating him?"

"Who?"

"The Mann."

"Oh my God, no! I told you, he's very involved with Pop Philly. And he's a nice guy. But we're not *involved*."

"If you say so."

"Pea?"

"Yes?"

"Are you okay?"

"I'm at work. I'm fine. I'm just trying to figure out how to do it all without screwing anything or anyone up."

"Look, I know this isn't what you want to be doing. But let yourself go. It'll be fun. You tell your stories and the rest will be easy."

"How do you know?"

"Am I ever wrong?"

"You want me to list them by name?"

"Uh, no thanks. You needed the distraction and I needed you. This was an untapped demographic and we tapped it. We've always been a great team. Look, I know that this is selective sharing. You're not telling everything about Mac or your own dating experiences, and that's *fine*. A girl's got to have her secrets."

I was lying to my best friend, putting her business at risk as well as risking losing her trust and possibly her friendship. Was it worth it? I had no way of knowing. Jade had agreed to this. It was her idea. Bloggers were anonymous all the time. Maybe they all conjured posts from their imaginations. How was anyone to know? Was there a moral code attached to blogging? I knew there was a moral code to life. I wasn't ditching it forever, just temporarily. Just enough time to figure out what I'd do if Bruce didn't come back. Or didn't pay child support again.

I felt woozy. My stomach flipped.

What I wanted was for Bruce to come home—*come back*—and for life to return to the new normal we'd created with my Wednesday nights and every other weekend off. I needed that time to dig myself out of the trenches. I didn't covet those times because I was away from Noah, but those times reinforced how much I wanted to be with Noah. Always. How becoming a mom was the best decision I'd made. Sometimes I thought it was the only good decision I'd made.

Yet I mentioned none of that in this first blog post. I'd revealed myself as a divorced mom who'd been dating. Who was in a relationship. For real. In the blog I had style and moxie. In real life, I simply had gall. A month or two and it would be over, a short chapter where I got what I needed and gave Jade, the readers—and Andrew "Coat Guy" Mann, who wrote the check—what they wanted.

"I have to go now," Jade said in a business voice I was starting to recognize. "I'll let you know when we can both sit down with Drew."

"Why?"

"Because he's interested in everything that happens with Pop Philly. I told you, we're friends. I just think the three of us should sit down and talk about the future. Your future and ours."

I sighed, which filled the time slot for my reply. "Maybe."

"It'll all turn out okay. You'll see. Am I ever wrong?" Jade said it with the same promise with which she'd told me that sleeping in youth hostels throughout Europe would enrich our character and that marrying Bruce would work out fine.

Yes. Sometimes Jade was wrong.

I opened the office door and waved at Donna, who turned to the line of waiting students. I hadn't even asked about Donna's weekend, or her mother in the hospital, or her latest obsession—online Scrabble. She tapped Bethany, a senior, on the back. Bethany stood up straight and tipped her shoulders back. Bethany was one of my favorite students, headed to West Chester University on a field hockey scholarship.

"What's going on with Marcus?" I asked as I shut the door.

"We broke up. He doesn't like that I'm going to live on campus when he's living at home and going to CCP."

I put my arm around Bethany's shoulder. "Don't let him guilt you into living at home. You're following your own dream. Not his. You do not need a boy for anything."

Bethany tilted her head and raised her eyebrows.

I tapped her arm. "None of that nonsense, young lady. You are on the right path. Just be true to yourself and everything will be fine."

"I know, Ms. Lane."

"And if you need a reason to stay after school and off that bus so you don't have to deal with him?"

"I can always come here and you'll find something for me to do. Yes. I know. But I'm cool."

"Well, don't forget."

I handed Bethany her signed papers and asked her to send in the next student.

Albert walked into my office with forms for Arcadia and Temple. "What are you going to write?"

"The truth, Mr. Jones. That's my job."

Irony speared me.

After Albert I met with a transfer student from Archbishop Henry, lectured a suspended Liberty student needing to go back to class, and admitted a new freshman from Turkmenistan, whose parents spoke no English, all followed by a midwinter fire drill.

I grabbed my phone—just in case. Just in case I had a moment during the trek outside, amidst the silent commotion, to count the comments on my blog.

— Chapter 10 —

Battleship

NOAH NESTLED THE PHONE in its cradle and cried.

"Aye, matey," I said in a soft mommy voice as I lifted him onto my lap. Nothing better than a La-Z-Boy for a snuggle.

"I know you miss your daddy." Noah just lay on me again, like the night before, and the night before that. He stuck his thumb in his mouth and I pulled it out and patted his hand as I dried it on my shirt. "He misses you a lot. I mean, like, gazillions."

"That's what he said." Noah picked up his head and looked at me, his spare, dark eyebrows furrowed.

I breathed him in, looked from his chin to his cheek, forehead, nose, cheek, and back to his chin. Then I looked into his eyes and buried my bubbling anger toward my ex.

"Moms and dads always miss their kids gazillions." I had no doubt Bruce missed our son, but that didn't mean I understood how he could go away, unable to reach out and touch Noah. My Noah. *Our* Noah. For the past two weeks he had cried, then sulked after Bruce's daily calls. It would take at least an hour for him to step out from my shadow. I wanted to tell Bruce to call every other day, not to interrupt the momentum we gained after school, through kindergarten cut-and-paste homework, dinner, and playtime. But I couldn't. The only thing I hoped is that the pain would ease for Noah, and increase for Bruce, propelling him back to Philly.

I kept at bay any thoughts that his absence might be longer than temporary.

"Pirates go on long adventures and miss their families very much, too. Just like Daddy."

Noah's eyes opened wide, brimming with newfound respect for Bruce. Not my intention, except when I saw Noah's smile.

My evenings had become routine in the comforting way. After Noah fell asleep, I'd amble downstairs to the kitchen and pull out the Phillies cap from amid my stacks of notes in the bread drawer. I'd already be wearing my old, but newly minted, writing clothes: plaid flannel pants, thinning navy Penn sweatshirt, and my one pair of SmartWool socks I'd purchased for my one Killington ski trip with Bruce. I'd make myself a cup of green tea, and at some point Felix would hop onto the keyboard.

Tonight I sipped my tea and clicked open *P-O-F,* rereading my latest post before heading into the comments section. After two weeks of being the official *Philly over Forty* maven, I didn't always remember everything I'd written or all the comments and how I responded. It was as if I stored this part of my life, my day, into its own little locker, separate from everything else.

But when I opened it . . . that was another story. The thoughts and words just tumbled out. I clicked and scrolled. Mac and I went out to dinner again. We'd gone to the movies. He was funny, attentive, and handsome (oh my!). He was busy with work and I was busy at school and with Noah. That was critical information for when I saw Rachel this coming weekend. That information would have to filter over to real life, because Rachel would ask. About everything. Why wasn't I going out with Mac when *she* would have offered to take Noah overnight? I'd just blame my social debacles on Bruce. Bruce was away, Noah was adjusting. Blah blah blah. Rachel wouldn't question my prioritizing time with Noah over time with Mac.

I skimmed the comments. Some were from online trolls posting links to counterfeit-luxury-handbag Web sites:

Chanell and Gucchie 80% off

Or too-good-to-be-true instant careers:

Make $400 a day stuffing envelopes at home like I did!

Some were snippets of other single parents' own divorce stories:

My ex is now dating a twenty-four-year-old.—Judith from Wyoming

At least Amber was thirty-five.

Some readers shared *special* dating advice:

Don't let this one get away like the other ones.—Ellen from New York

Wyoming? New York? I knew Web sites had no geographical boundaries, but why was anyone anywhere else reading *Philly over Forty*?

Some readers asked for dating advice:

How soon is too soon to call my new boyfriend my boyfriend?—Alice in Baltimore

I'm glad you asked, Alice. But I have no idea.

And some readers' comments made me think. Maybe more than I wanted to:

My ex wasn't right for me. The last guy I dated wasn't right for me. I'm forty-one. How do I figure out what kind of guy is right for me?—Fern in Chicago

Invent him.

That Sunday I didn't have to invent anything. I just had to hang out with Rachel and the kids in the real world. It was Rachel's world where we'd be hanging out, and I liked it there. It reminded me of what was possible. A happy marriage, a full minivan, realized dreams.

Rachel lifted her laptop from the old-barn-wood-now-new-coffee-table and placed it on her knees so I could see the monitor. Even in the house, just waiting for me, she wore a heather-gray cotton knit dress and purple tights. Rachel could always answer the door or leave home on a whim. I, in my *good* yoga pants, had barricaded myself into the corner of her family-room sectional. My arm slid across the microfiber cushion. The sensation was light and ticklish, but unwelcome, like a spider. I pulled down my sleeve.

"So, what's it like to be famous?" Rachel asked.

"I'm not famous."

"You're totally famous." She clicked on a tab and the *Philly over Forty* page appeared across her monitor. And there I was. Hidden for the world to see under my pixelated cap.

Rachel's middle finger slid across the touch pad and she tapped, opening up my latest post.

"Look at all those comments! And they're from everywhere, did you notice? And the ads?" She pointed to the sidebar. "That Andrew Mann is everywhere. Did you see that new animated billboard on 95?"

I had not.

"And you're totally helping all these people figure out their own dating stuff. It's so cool. Let's read them. I can be your assistant." She clapped her hands together. "I'll read the comments out loud and can tell you which ones you want to answer. I'm going to read every post and every comment anyway."

Rachel looked at me and smiled, her deep dimple revealing itself in her freckled left cheek. I envied those freckles as a child. Now I was glad I didn't have to worry about covering them with foundation. Otherwise, I coveted Rachel's life. But I didn't want her not to have it.

"It's okay to be proud of yourself, you know." She bumped me with her shoulder. "It's pretty awesome. The Internet is amazing."

"I have to tell you something."

"Oh, good! I have to tell you something, too."

"You go first!" we yelled in unison, each pointing at the other. Then we burst out laughing, Rachel's head landing on my shoulder, our bellies rising and falling in time to our chuckles and heaves. We did that often as children, said the same thing at the same time. And now, like then, every time our chuckles slowed, our breathing softened, one of us started again with an eruption of overzealous squeals. My side hurt with the joyful release of stress. Every time we looked at each other we started again, the way we did during long seder dinners when we were supposed to be quiet, or even at Saturday-morning services, where the *alter kockers* gave us the evil eye.

"Tell me about Mac."

"You know about Mac."

"For real, tell me. Don't make me read about him. What's he like? What do you like about him? I know you don't want me to meet him yet, I understand you're being cautious, but you can tell me something, can't you?"

Surely Rachel would understand why I lied about Mac, why I kept up the deception longer than I'd intended. We could always look across her mother's dining-room table and know what the other was thinking. Just a glance and one of us would ask to be excused or distract her father while the other took extra cookies. I looked at Rachel and saw the little girl of countless sleepovers in her basement. I wanted Rachel to know what I was going through. Why couldn't she look at me and just *know*?

"You think about it—and I'll go first this time," she said as if she'd just run a marathon.

"No, let me go first, it's really important." I grabbed her hand to stop her from tapping on the keyboard.

"So is this." She looked over her shoulder toward the playroom where all the kids were entrenched in LEGO. Rachel pivoted the laptop toward me. She never asked to go first. It was her turn. "I'm planning my reunion, right?"

"Riiiight." Rachel was a year younger than me, so our milestones were always a year apart, which made it fun. Bat mitzvahs, proms, graduations. Mine always came first . . . until it came to weddings. But then I got back in the groove with my divorce. With that I wouldn't be first, I'd be only. "You want to talk about your reunion now?"

"Not just the reunion. Look."

I stared at the monitor and there he was. Jeremy Goldfarb. Rachel's boyfriend from high school, college, and beyond stared back at me from his high school graduation photo, his eighteen-year-old eyes half-hidden by nineties-guy bangs.

"Everyone finds old boyfriends online, Rache. Are you going to tell me you've never looked for Jeremy before?"

"He wasn't on Facebook until a few weeks ago. I'm not online all the time like you, missy."

Really? Then how was it that every time I looked on

Facebook she had posted a new photo? "Great, he'll go to the reunion and Seth can see the boy who tormented you for ten years before you met him."

"Seth's not going to the reunion."

"Why?"

"I told him I'd be too busy and he'd have no one to hang out with."

It was probably true. "So do you think *he'll* go?" I was pretty sure that Rachel's first love, Jeremy Goldfarb, had lasted until the day she met Seth. Maybe longer.

"Of course *he'll* go; he's on the committee." She rose from the sofa in one fluid motion. "Should we give the kids lunch?"

"Wait." I stood and grabbed Rachel's arm. I swung her around toward me as if we were competing on *Dancing with the Stars*. "You're in touch with Jeremy Goldfarb?"

She turned away and sighed. Sighed!

"Rachel, don't you turn your back on me." I almost said *young lady*. "What is going on?"

"Nothing. We're just friends. It's nice to be in touch."

"Since when?"

"Since we started planning the reunion."

"I thought *you* were planning your reunion."

"You don't think I'm doing it alone, do you? There has to be a committee and Jeremy offered to be my cochair."

"What does Seth think of this?"

"He doesn't care."

"He doesn't *care* or he doesn't *know*?"

"He doesn't know but he wouldn't care."

"Rachel, you wouldn't have shown me this unless there was

something you wanted me to know. You're not random or casual. You're very deliberate. You think everything through."

Rachel scurried to the kitchen and I followed at her heels. Without talking, we gathered cold elbow noodles out of the fridge and a box of chicken nuggets from the freezer. I sliced green apples. Rachel ran cold water into the noodles in a colander and juggled plastic plates, juice boxes, and colorful silverware. She multitasked as if an octopus.

"He's married, Iz."

"You're married, too."

"Oh, thanks for the reminder." She slid nuggets into the convection oven, poked straws through juice pouches, and dealt plates, napkins, and colorful kid silverware onto the kids' table. Every action seemed to punctuate her statement with sarcasm. "Because making dinner for six people every night, four of whom complain about it, and driving a van that seats eight and can turn into Disneyland with the touch of a button isn't enough of a reminder."

"All you ever wanted was a minivan full of kids. It's all *we* ever wanted." I stepped back, away from her, almost sitting on the kitchen table.

"No, it's what *you* wanted. A picnic table with boys on one side and girls on the other, all dressed in OshKosh overalls with you sitting at the foot of the table and your imaginary husband sitting at the head of it. How's that working out for you?"

I stopped moving, and not just at the mention of my "imaginary husband." I stopped because she had slammed the truth over my head.

"I'm sorry, that was mean."

That it was. But it was also true. "You're right. That was mean. I'm a daydreamer. I want things I don't have. I want people I don't have. I don't even mean Bruce. I mean the life, the kids, the plans." The words had a bitter aftertaste. I had never before said them aloud. Now I knew why. They tasted rancid.

"I'm sorry. I'm just stressed. And it's an escape, that's all. Planning something that is just for me and has nothing to do with Seth or the kids. It's been a long time. I don't get time off from parenting, or a new, exciting relationship, like you do."

"Noah hasn't seen Bruce in weeks! Do you know what that's like? And there's never really time off when you're a mom, no matter who you are. You know that. And as for a new, exciting anything . . ."

She stopped fussing with the food and turned to me, eyes wide.

"It's not all it's cracked up to be. So I'm pretty sure you don't want it."

Rachel put her arm around my waist. "I'm sorry."

I kissed the top of her head. I could never stay mad at her.

"I have another one of those stupid hospital black-tie things next weekend," Rachel returned to her job of fixing lunch. "Maybe you and Mac could come. Seth could get extra tickets."

"I don't think so."

"Why not? You could leave Noah here with my kids and the sitter. He'd have a blast."

"I'm just not ready to go public with Mac."

"You're not ready to go public? Do you know how ridiculous that sounds?"

I shrugged. Fake Mac had a little social anxiety. "Next time, maybe?"

"Deal, but I'm going to hold you to it. There's something in June . . ."

"If I'm still with Mac, I'll put it on my calendar."

Rachel turned back to the oven. "I know you don't want to hear me complain about getting dressed up and going out, but it's not fun like going out on dates with a new guy, when everything is exciting. This is an obligation. And if you haven't noticed, I don't have my pre-baby body back yet." She looked down, from one hip to the other.

What Rachel didn't say was that she had never had the quintessential pre-baby body and that Arielle, her youngest, was three years old.

"Those are new." I pointed with my chin to a small collection of plants nestled close together on the windowsill. In the middle of winter. "Are those herbs?"

"They are."

The oven dinged and I grabbed the ketchup and honey mustard from the fridge and wiped the insides of the lids even though they were clean. Sometimes I imagined Rachel with a stockroom full of new bottles purchased just for me. It was more likely that we'd both inherited the Lane aversion to condiment crust.

"Lunchtime!"

Rachel held the doorjamb the way her mother had held on to the windowsill and called to us years ago. That moment echoed a time filled with white bread and peanut butter and inappropriate language in front of children. When the grown-ups sputtered in whispered, broken Yiddish, the language of their grandparents, just so we wouldn't understand, when in reality we didn't care what they were saying.

Our own kids gathered on the sunporch, heated for winter, and we sat in the kitchen gobbling leftover Chinese with pull-apart chopsticks. No white bread, no Yiddish.

I looked through and beyond our five offspring, out at the covered pool and wide-open, bright winter sky. When I looked out the window onto Good Street, I saw row houses. If I looked up, I saw my personal rectangle of sky. I had always wanted a bigger piece of sky, and I'd always had it at Rachel's. I never begrudged her the breadth of her view, but today it reminded me of what I didn't have. And it reminded me of what she could lose if she went down an online black hole with Jeremy.

"Jeremy is still really funny." Rachel stood and leaned into the basil. She left her nose in the leaves, but shifted to the parsley, as if it would agree.

A swirl of panic circled my middle. "Exactly how often do you talk to him?"

"I don't talk to him. We message. Online. It's not a big deal. It's all about the reunion." Her words were quick, strung together without a breath, yet they sounded rehearsed. Of course Rachel knew what she'd say to me. She was a planner.

"Why don't you tell him you don't need his help?"

"But I do."

"Rache, no."

"It's a reunion, Iz."

Deliberate name abbreviations were always a sign of trouble between us.

"What kind of reunion?"

"Knock it off."

My phone buzzed.

"Who's that? Is it Mac? Oh, I wish you would tell me his real name! Answer it. I want to hear his voice! He doesn't have to know!"

"No!" I grabbed my phone and walked headfirst into the corner. Head down, I scrolled through the texts and alerts. Jade/Pop Philly/Ethan/Jade again. I was never going to get anything done if they didn't leave me alone.

"What is going on with Mac?"

"Nothing is going on with Mac. I just forgot to shut off my phone. Now, where were we? Right. Jeremy. We were talking about *you*."

"I thought you'd get a kick out of me reconnecting with Jeremy after all this time."

Yes, a kick in the gut.

I knew how time dissolved in the moment it took to share a memory. I hit my cousin with my *Are you crazy?* stare the way I did the first time she added grape juice into the Manischewitz bottle after we drank it. "This is dangerous, Rache. You can't have a relationship with your old boyfriend."

"Izzy. There is nothing going on." She twirled on one foot and landed hard. "I love Seth. And, in case this scene has escaped your line of vision, I have four kids and a mortgage and a Disney vacation villa with Seth."

"I know you. You wouldn't have shown me the photo if it weren't important to you. And you didn't answer me. How often do you talk to him?"

"I talk to Seth every day." She rolled her eyes. "I don't know how often I talk to him. I don't count because it's not important. Does *that* answer your question?"

"What do you mean, you don't count? There's enough to count? Once a week? Twice a week? On Wednesdays at six?"

"A few times a day."

"A few times a day?" I shuddered as a chill ran up my arms. "Rachey. You need to stop. These things lead to trouble."

"Oh my God, Iz. The Internet is your saving grace now that Bruce is gone, but it's *my* danger zone? Why were there different rules for you than for me? Since forever. I'm excited about something, I'm having fun. Why can't you be happy for me?"

Rachel was an only child. She looked up to me. She idealized my parents' owning a store as if we sold kittens and cotton candy instead of nuts and bolts and Con-Tact paper.

"You're excited about your class reunion or you're excited about your reunion with Jeremy Goldfarb?"

"Both."

Finally an honest answer. "Whatever you think you have with Jeremy, Rachel, it isn't real. The Internet isn't real. He can be who he wants and tell you anything you want to hear. Trust me." The words burned in my throat.

"What kind of person do you think he is?"

"I don't know. And neither do you. Maybe he's not married. Maybe he has a criminal record."

"He's some kind of engineer and he lives in Cherry Hill. He's one of the good guys. And we're not doing anything wrong. We're just *talking*. What's your problem?"

"My problem is that people lie. That's all." There was my

opening. I clamped my lips to close it. This was about Rachel now, not me.

She waved her hands like shooing a bug. "People post flattering pictures of themselves and happy family snapshots, but people don't just lie. They don't say they went to Paris for the weekend when they're really holed up in King of Prussia Mall. And—I'm not lying about Jeremy. I just told you I was back in touch with him."

"Are you lying to Seth?"

"No."

Absolute delusion ran in our family.

I added ice to a glass and slid it across my forehead. Rachel was lying to Seth. I knew it. And I was lying to her. And everyone else. Why was it easy for me to want to untangle the knot in her life but not my own? And why did I demand honesty but not return it? Why was it sometimes so hard to do what was good and right?

I could leave Rachel on her disastrous course, or I could help her through this, redirect her attention to something. Or someone. *Me.* I came to Rachel's with the intention of a playdate for Noah and a confession for me. If I told her I had a problem, needed her help, her attention, her time, maybe that would help her *and* me.

"I promise," Rachel said. "This is about a class reunion, not a clandestine meeting. It's just about me having fun. For once, something is just about me."

My thoughts became malleable. "Nothing's just about you anymore, is it?"

"Nope."

"Four kids and a husband and a house . . ." I breathed deep. "And planning a reunion. That's a lot."

"It is."

"But you do a lot. You play mah-jongg and tennis. You're on committees. Those are for you. And if they're not, you should stop."

"It wouldn't look right. All of this comes with an image."

I'd never thought of Rachel as caring what anyone thought. She seemed to embrace her traditional life, and all its trimmings.

"And talking to your high school boyfriend is part of that image?"

Rachel shrugged. "It's a distraction. Sometimes I want to forget about what I'm making for dinner or what I'm wearing to that stupid black-tie thing or who I'm supposed to meet where and at what time. And since you won't distract me with more stories about Mac . . ."

"Do not blame me!"

Rachel's face, which rounded with each smile, grew long and sullen. She handed me a symmetrically arranged bundle of basil, oregano, and cilantro tied together with a stem.

"See? You *love* the whole domestic-goddess/doctor's-wife thing."

"No, I don't. Not always."

Now I prayed she *was* lying.

Chapter 11

Whisper Down the Lane

I AGREED TO MEET Ethan at the Oxford Diner because I thought we'd be having breakfast at the diner of our childhoods. I anticipated the mauve vinyl booths with duct-taped tears and nicked wood-grain laminate tabletops. Instead, the booths had been refurbished with taupe vinyl seats—as if taupe outranked mauve—and beige laminate tabletops with flecks of gold. All much too pristine for my memories. "The Oxford" had been the only restaurant my parents took me to as a child. I learned table manners here. Napkin on lap. Elbows off table. Salad fork, dinner fork, soupspoon, teaspoon. When my brothers were with us, Eddie ate a full-course meat-and-potatoes meal, while Ethan ordered something exotic sounding that no one wanted to taste but me. Because of Ethan I ate moussaka, veal marsala, and eggplant Parmesan before I was ten. Dad always ordered a corned beef "special," while Mom opted for whitefish on a poppy-seed bagel or a cantaloupe stuffed with cottage cheese. I ate a Texas Tommy because, although my parents didn't keep a kosher home, pork products did not cross its threshold. Today I'd get sick from a ballpark-style hot dog with melted American cheese and bacon, but as a kid? It was heaven on a plate with a side of fries.

Mmm. Fries.

"An order of fries, too, please."

The order was almost the same as my late-night orders during high school: bagel and cream cheese, order of fries, and a black-and-white shake.

I couldn't. Could I?

I looked at the waitress's name tag, pinned to her chest like a badge of honor. "And a black-and-white milk shake."

Tanya smiled and removed a pen from her apron pocket. "What kind of bagel? Toasted? Light? Dark? What kind of cream cheese? Plain, chive, veggie, light, lox, honey-walnut? What kind of fries? Regular, seasoned, waffle, or sweet potato?"

When had everything become so complicated?

"Are you going to drink that water or be hypnotized by it?" I stopped staring at my ice cubes and looked up at Ethan. He hadn't shaved, and his polo shirt was a little rumpled, his coat on his arm in a heap. Apparently my brother was enjoying an occasional day off from dapper.

I leapt from the booth and pummeled him with a hug.

"I'm happy to see you, too, Iz."

We slid into our places on opposite sides. Ethan looked at Tanya. Then at me. Then back at Tanya, who smiled, revealing a sizable gap between her two front teeth.

"Did she order a black-and-white shake?"

Tanya nodded.

"And a bagel and fries?"

Tanya smiled again at Ethan, then at me, double-lifting her penciled-in eyebrows as if to say, *Wow, he knows you.*

"Sesame bagel, toasted, plain cream cheese, regular fries," I said.

"I'll share hers," Ethan said.

I harrumphed. Tanya scribbled on her order pad, nodded, and walked away.

Ethan propped his elbows on the table, sank his chin into his hands. I smiled at his attempt to cheer me without knowing what was wrong. If anything was wrong. I also laughed because somewhere in Margate our mother was having an inexplicable bad-manners twinge.

Ethan looked around and stared at the brass light fixture hanging over the booth. "What did I miss?"

"Well, I almost ordered the waffle fries . . ."

"Very funny."

My phone buzzed and I tucked it under my leg. "I should've told you sooner, but Bruce went to California. With a girl. I mean, his girlfriend, Amber."

"Damn."

Ethan had known that something was going on. I had texted him to meet me when I dropped off Noah for Sunday school, and because I knew that his daughter, Maya, was spending the weekend with our parents. He hadn't asked where to meet. He just knew.

Tanya placed everything in the middle of the table, unsure what belonged to whom. I knew, as did Ethan, that we would share everything even-steven.

Ethan squirted a blob of ketchup along the edge of the

french-fry plate. He plucked one from the center and pointed it at me. I took the bottle and opened the lid to wipe it clean, but he closed it and slid the ketchup to the side. A clean-condiment calamity.

"Why do you care what Bruce does and who he does it with?" Ethan's voice was like my own; I heard it from the inside out. "You need to move on, too, you know."

"He lost his job and now he's in California with his girlfriend, and he's not paying child support or doing anything but talking with Noah, which is not like taking him for a night or a weekend." Pause for breath. "E, I'm not supposed to be doing this alone."

Ethan's eyes widened. He dug in his pocket and pulled out his phone. "I'll call Eddie. We'll get Bruce's sorry ass back here."

It comforted me to think of my brothers rushing to my defense. "Don't." I reached across the table and put my hand on his, my elbow almost skimming the ketchup. "I told him I'd give him time to figure things out."

"You're not getting back together with Bruce, Iz."

"I know that."

"Are you sure?"

I did know. Usually.

"I hate to ask this, but how can you pay your bills without that support? You're legally entitled to child support until Noah is eighteen. And, not to be cliché, but I know you don't use that money to buy bonbons."

Ethan did know. He was the one who'd convinced me to move home, helped me plan a budget, and who, with Jade and Rachel, packed up half of a married life.

"Do you want a loan? I assume you won't ask Eddie. Or Mom and Dad."

"No, I won't. You know that. And I don't want a loan." My heart and voice softened. "But thank you."

"Well, how about a gift? I can do that; I'm your big brother. Consider it an early fortieth-birthday present!"

"I'm fine. Really." I sat straighter. "I—got a part-time job! I work from home, at night, when Noah is asleep."

"Do *not* tell me you are one of the 1-900 operators." I knew Ethan was kidding. I hoped Ethan was kidding.

"You know Jade's Web site?"

"I don't really read it, but everyone has heard of Pop Philly."

"I'm the new *Philly over Forty* blogger."

"No!" Ethan crashed back on the booth, mouth open.

"Yes!" I'd impressed my impressive big brother.

"Well, why didn't you tell me? We should celebrate! Do Mom and Dad know? Did you tell Eddie? Trish is going to have an absolute cow!"

"No one knows."

"What do you mean no one knows? This is huge!"

"I'm anonymous."

"Ooh!" Then he whispered, "I mean, *ooh*!"

"It's fun," I said at a normal decibel level. Whispering garnered more attention than talking.

"*Philly over Forty,* huh? What are you writing about exactly?"

Ethan was anti-secret. He came out of the closet at twenty-one and had little tolerance for pretending. If he knew the truth, he would likely wince with disappointment.

I bit into my bagel to muffle my response. "Being forty—almost—about dating mostly. All about dating over forty, about my relationships, that kind of thing."

"I'm not sure that handful—and I mean that figuratively—of guys you went out with right after Bruce left really qualify as relationships."

"That's just a detail."

"Izzy!"

I swallowed my bagel and smiled a deliberate smile. Extra-wide even for a Lane.

Ethan took my hand and channeled our mother. "If I wanted the CliffsNotes, I would have bought them."

I told him everything.

Everything.

And what a relief that was.

Ethan tapped on his phone, downloaded the Pop Philly mobile app, and subscribed to my posts. He scrolled through the pages, the comments, and stopped at the photo of the Phillies cap.

"Is *this* actually you?"

I nodded.

"Well, that's one thing. I will look at all of this at home, but I know one thing for sure. You're going to get into trouble."

"It's fine."

"Nothing about it is fine. You're writing about a boyfriend you don't have and dates you haven't gone on, and people think it's real. You can't tell your family. Not because you don't want the public to know your identity, but because you can't have the people who love you think you're doing all these things.

You're giving dating advice. When was the last date you actually went on?"

"Just because I'm not dating doesn't mean I can't give advice. I'm helping the kids at Liberty get into college and I haven't done that since, when? Nineteen ninety-two?" I dipped a fry into my milk shake. "And speaking of relationships, our Rachel is talking to *Jeremy Goldfarb* online."

"Her high school boyfriend? Wow. What'd she do, look him up on Facebook?" Rerouting successful. "Hey, don't change the subject. We're talking about you. She is not my sister."

"That's not very nice."

"You are a priority to me. Plus, she has Seth to take care of her. You have . . ."

"No one. Thanks, Ethan. Thanks for your confidence and support." I threw my napkin onto the table.

"Let me support you by giving you some money so you don't have to do this."

"I'm not taking money from you. I'm living in my parents' house because I couldn't afford to live anywhere else after my husband left me in our fixer-upper dream house. And if that's not humiliating enough, he took off for California with his girlfriend a year after saying he wanted to 'find himself' and didn't want a 'serious relationship,' leaving all his responsibilities for money and Noah behind. I'm not running away from this, E. Bruce is the one who runs. I'm the one who stays. I need to take care of us without your help. Without any help. It's not that I want to—I need to. I need to do this, no matter what it takes."

That was it. I heard the words inside my head once and then

again as they flew through the air toward my brother. I wanted to reach out and catch them, hold them, then stuff them into my pocket so I didn't forget my momentary resolve. I didn't want a handout or a loan or even a gift, although I would let Ethan pay for breakfast. I had never intended to be a divorced mom with one son living in the house where I grew up, hanging out with a beloved aging next-door neighbor on a street that wasn't what we needed or remembered. Yet that's exactly where I was. Whether proving I could take care of Noah and myself was for me or Bruce or Ethan or the world, or all of us, I didn't know. And it didn't matter.

"I'm just worried this is going to jump up and bite you when everyone finds out."

"No one is going to find out, Ethan."

"These things have a way of coming out."

We snorted.

When Ethan came out, at least to our parents, me, and Eddie, he physically lined us up on the sofa and drew the curtains. In retrospect, I'm surprised he didn't play mood music. Ethan liked theatrics. "I'm gay," he said, "and there's nothing you can do about it." I was eleven, it was the eighties, and I had no solid idea of what *gay* meant except for "happy." Ethan looked happy, which was all I had cared about. Therefore, in the infancy of AIDS awareness and gay rights, all I knew was that gay was okay with me. I didn't realize how big of a deal it was that there was no pushback, or a faux shivah, from my parents. They said, "Okay, Ethan." And that was that. It was much more of a *shanda*, an embarrassment, when Eddie brought Patty from Fishtown home for Passover later that year. No one in our family had ever dated a gentile, not to mention someone from what would be considered the wrong side of the tracks. Patty was a twofer. While my blog buddy, Holden, might have been mired in the revitalized hipster culture of Fishtown, in 1988 Patricia Kathleen Bernadette O'Brien was just a shiksa from a bad neighborhood.

Of course, now Patty was Trish, and we loved her.

I didn't know it at Eddie and Trish's wedding when I was fourteen, but it was then that my parents officially pinned their dream of a Jewish wedding and Jewish grandchildren on me. I still felt that prick. In more ways than one.

"So, just let me clarify," Ethan said. "Jade doesn't know that you're making this guy up."

"Right."

"And she needs you to write this blog for her site. It's important to her."

"Right."

"How can Jade not know? She knows everything about you."

"She doesn't know!"

"She doesn't want to meet this guy? What's his name again?"

"Mac."

"Mac what?"

"Oh my God, E. Just Mac. Stop."

"And Rachel doesn't know?"

"No! No one knows. Not true. Mrs. Feldman knows. And *she's* not going to tell anyone." I waggled my finger.

"This could go on forever, Iz. What are you going to do? Marry a make-believe groom? Have some invisible babies?"

He grabbed my hand and the familiar touch felt like the hated childhood game of Chinese finger trap. I tugged and he held tighter, and the weight of elapsed dreams squeezed. Ethan released me and slid the plate of fries in front of us to my side of the table. He knew about my big-family, picnic-table dreams.

"Can we change the subject? Show me new pictures of my niece."

Ethan slid his phone to me. He had adopted Maya six months before, and there she was in a hot-pink parka with white faux-fur trim, looking at me with gray-green eyes. Her hair was shorter than mine, black as ink against her pecan-colored skin. I loved Eddie and Trish's kids, but Brooke and Matthew were adults at twenty and twenty-six. When Matthew was born, I was busy becoming a teenager. By the time Brooke was born, I was busy with college, dating, and my own ambitions. But Maya arrived at just the right time. For all of us.

I returned the favor and shared the latest photos of Noah.

"We have great kids," Ethan said. "And we need to set good examples. I'm not sure this qualifies."

So much for changing the subject. The fries were cold but I ate them anyway.

"You do not want to start your forties off on the wrong foot. Maybe you just need a plan. How about getting out of this by your birthday? New decade. Clean slate. What do you say? Then we can really celebrate your birthday in style."

I scanned the calendar in my head. In about six weeks I'd be forty. Four zero. Surely Bruce would be back, and employed, and I could wean myself off *Philly over Forty*. By then I'd probably be tired of all the attention anyway. Doubt poked me but I ignored it.

I didn't have the heart or the stomach to tell Ethan how much different parts of *P-O-F* suited me, how getting lost in the ether of the Internet patched holes in my days and my heart. Comments popped up at all hours, from all over the country, reminding me how it felt to be listened to instead of talked at. As soon as a new post went live on the site, it was tweeted and Facebooked and Tumblred. My recent post about sex after divorce, with no mention of Mac, went viral with more views than anything else on Pop Philly ever. It was peculiar to be popular. Peculiar in a heart-pounding, ego-boosting, anonymous kind of way.

But Ethan was right. Whatever I did affected Noah. He deserved to grow up in an honest home. I couldn't let him grow up with me telling lies—online *or* to myself.

I reached for my brother's hands across the table and held them tight, but not too tight, over the empty french-fry plate.

"I'll figure this out by my birthday. You've got a deal."

Chapter 12
Bombardment

Noah stomped traces of snow from his sneakers, causing Mrs. Feldman's dining room étagère to shake. I had forgotten how temperamental her Lladró collection was, how many times growing up I'd pushed the door shut a little too hard and then trembled as I heard the joggling of porcelain ballerinas and harlequins. I mouthed, *Sorry.*

"I love that rattling, Elizabeth. It sounds like life to me." Mrs. Feldman waved her hand as if swatting at bees. "It reminds me of when my boys were running in and out and through the house all day long. And when *you* were running in and out of this house."

She looked over my shoulder and glanced toward the floor, as if little girl me were standing there, ready to unpack her Calico Critters. Mrs. Feldman smiled and shook her head. That seemed to bring her back to the present. She tugged on Noah's coat sleeve, more like a playmate than a surrogate grandmother, and he shimmied out of it, revealing a sweatshirt with a skull and crossbones, something I wouldn't let him wear to school.

"Did you eat your dinner, Mr. Pirate?"

"Arrr."

"There are cookies and a juice box in the living room, and the TV is set to your favorite channel. Just use the clicker to turn it on."

Noah looked at me and I tipped my head.

With the coats over the banister and the shoes tucked against the wall, Mrs. Feldman and I walked to the kitchen. Without a word I grabbed a Brillo pad from under the sink and started scrubbing a pot that was soaking. What had she been cooking? And for whom?

"Did I miss a party?" I was only half kidding.

"Just some *prokas* for the boys. I packed it up so they can freeze it. None of my daughters-in-law make it. Never have." Mrs. Feldman shrugged, baffled by the aversion to stuffed cabbage.

I rinsed the pot, then turned around. "I told Ethan about Mac."

"And?"

I shook my head. "He wasn't happy."

"Stop scrubbing and come sit."

I dried my hands on a dish towel one finger at a time. A buzzing lightness came over me. Where had my diner determination gone?

"I'm not telling you what to do, Elizabeth. I just wonder how you're writing about dating when those dates of yours were really nothing to write home about. That first fellow wanted you to bring Noah on your date."

"I forgot about that guy!" It was true. The assumption that

I was a "package deal" with my five-year-old son was disconcerting. I wouldn't become a package-anything until I knew someone was not an ax murderer/child molester/porn addict.

"Don't change the subject, Elizabeth. What's the plan? You must have a plan."

Mrs. Feldman never struck me as a schemer. But she'd drawn up her will when Mr. Feldman died twenty years ago. That was a definite plan she wasn't willing to alter. Her voice rose and her hands reached for mine. Hers were below-normal body temperature even though she kept the heat at a tropical seventy-six.

"The plan is that I'll write for Jade until Bruce is back and paying support again."

"And you don't think if you told Jade that she'd still find a place for you?"

"This is what she wants. She told me. She needs me to do this and do it this way."

"So she's paying you to lie to her readers? That's not good business for her or for you."

Cut to the chase, why don't you? "She doesn't know the truth and right now it's better that way."

"Better for who? You or Jade?"

"For both of us." I had to believe that. "If you read the Web site, you'd see . . . I'm really steering away from out-and-out lies." Mostly.

"I did read it, Elizabeth. I may not have wanted that computer Ray offered to buy for me, but I do go on the Internet at the library. You tell very wonderful stories. But they're stories. And saying you're lying to protect someone else? That's the classic liar's creed. Just admit that you're doing it to protect yourself."

"Jade will be hurt if I tell her the truth."

Mrs. Feldman placed her hands on her hips. "Really, Elizabeth. I expect more from you."

"Fine! I'm protecting myself, too."

Some lies were acceptable. I needed to believe that. Didn't everyone have acceptable lies as part of their life? How many people were really *fine* when asked? How many people *don't mind* doing what they're asked? How many people don't really look fat in jeans at least sometimes?

"Do you want to be good at lying, Elizabeth? So good that it just becomes part of your life, part of your being? Elizabeth?"

I wished she'd stop using my name. The four syllables spun like the aura of a migraine. I had never minded that she called me Elizabeth, but now it sounded harsh and accusatory. Izzy, on the other hand, sounded fun.

"I don't know. I mean, no. I just have to do this for now. Until my birthday. And that's the only plan I have." I couldn't think beyond tonight, getting Noah into bed, taking out my lists, writing my next post. Planning out my whole life had gotten me nowhere. "This keeps me busy when Noah is asleep, and I'm making up the money I'm not getting from Bruce. And I'm not lying about *everything*. My thoughts and feelings, those are real." And those thoughts and feelings were helping people. Entertaining them. Encouraging them to move forward. Even when I couldn't, and knew it.

I fiddled with my fingers, fidgety from the pressure on my psyche. I had been trained to problem solve, although much of that involved filling out paperwork and following instructions. I rationalized everything away. What did Mrs. Feldman know about this kind of thing anyway? She'd spent her adult life on Good Street, smoking Virginia Slims until well after I left for college. She stayed married to the same man for decades. She wrangled children, arranged flowers, and organized just about everything and everyone. And now she was the maven of the over-eighty crowd at shul and the JCC. This was not a woman who knew of lies and secrets. Her life was like her front door—wide-open even when it should be locked.

"This lying, it's worth it for the money and attention?"

"Yes, it is. For now."

"It's never just for now. You need to stop. Jade is your best friend and she will understand if you tell her now. But if you wait, you will become a snowball."

"You mean that the lie will snowball?"

"No, Elizabeth. I mean it just like I said it. You will become packed tight like a snowball, Elizabeth. Cold and hard. That's what lies will do to you."

"Not always." I almost called her Geraldine but it got stuck in my throat. "Anyway, it's more complicated than that."

"It always is."

Noah stood in the kitchen doorway with a stack of construction paper.

"What did you make?" I said.

"Pictures for Daddy." He held up the pile for me to see.

"Do you want to tell Mrs. Feldman what you're doing this weekend?"

"I'm having a sleepover with Cousin Maya. Can I go watch more TV?"

"Yes," I said. "But we're leaving soon. It's almost bedtime."

Noah walked away and I turned toward Mrs. Feldman.

"I don't know what I'll do with a night to myself since presumably I have a boyfriend and will be out on the town." Or swinging from an imaginary chandelier.

"Well, don't sit in front of your computer all night. Take advantage of the fact that Noah will be with Ethan and Maya." Mrs. Feldman ran her right hand over her left, as if brushing something away. "Your brother, it's quite something, the way he adopted Maya like that."

Like what? It was the first time since I'd moved home that Mrs. Feldman had mentioned Ethan's adopting Maya. I'd told her all about it six months ago, but didn't know if Mrs. Feldman struggled with the adoption itself, or if it was because Ethan was gay. Or because Maya wasn't white. Or born Jewish. I wasn't accustomed to Mrs. Feldman's silence, or its implied disapproval of my brother.

"Ethan is a great dad. He's loving and kind and funny. And he is giving Maya amazing opportunities she wouldn't have had if she stayed in foster care. Forget that, he loves her to pieces. It's like they were made for each other. And believe me, he'd say she's the one who's giving everything to him." I understood that completely.

"Oh, Elizabeth, I didn't mean anything bad. I mean that it's not the way it used to be. Nowadays you don't have to be married or part of a Norman Rockwell painting to be a family." Her voice was monotone; she stared out the window, then looked up and down the street a few times. "I think it's wonderful for them, really I do."

For once, I didn't believe her.

Chapter 13

I Spy

Two weeks until Valentine's Day and I had *nothing.* No ideas for how to blog about prix-fixe dinner reservations, itchy lace lingerie, heart-shaped boxes of mystery chocolates, or overpriced floral arrangements. I knew what the *P-O-F* readers wanted, and it tugged at my guiltstrings. They wanted *hope.* Because if it could happen for me, it could happen for them.

I read three extra books to Noah, tucked him in, and cleaned the bathroom. Then I donned my flannel pants, Penn sweatshirt, wool socks, and Phillies cap and settled onto the sofa with Felix behind my head.

I spent a high-speed hour and a half watching costumed and choreographed marriage proposals on YouTube, all in the name of research. When Mac proposed, he'd do it in private. Maybe with Noah by his side. I clicked on a bridal Web site and scanned wedding dresses. I'd want romantic and flowy, maybe with lace. I'd go with ivory since my first wedding dress was white. Maybe I'd get a different dress for the reception, something short and flirty. The possibilities were endless since the imaginary budget was too. I slammed the laptop and stood. What was I doing?

With freshly brewed tea and Felix now at my feet, I hovered the cursor over my *P-O-F* bookmark. Back to my version of reality. I clicked away, and instead of my usual landing page, I landed somewhere else. A red, white, and blue splash page beckoned: "C'mon, Philly over Forty: Be Part of the Conversation."

I slumped and I smiled. My bloggy banter in the comment section with the readers was a hit. Jade and Andrew might have wanted me to ramble, but they realized I knew what I was doing. The readers didn't need my stories as much as they needed to tell their own. I wondered what Bruce and Amber were doing. Was he as anti-romantic now as he had been with me? Or was I his only recipient of last-minute gifts and supermarket flowers? Then I knew. I didn't have to tell the readers about Valentine's Day. I could ask the readers *about* Valentine's Day.

I backtracked and logged on behind the scenes, on the page designated just for me, accessible only with my password. I typed my shortest ever *Philly over Forty* post:

What was your worst Valentine's Day? Your best?

A lot of sharing, and a little kvetching, would ensue. And I wouldn't have to lie.

I turned my cap backward and wrote two more blog posts. Even if there had been a Mac, I wouldn't be obsessed, I was too old for that. We'd have our own lives and friends and hobbies and interests. We'd respect each other's alone time, too. So without mentioning Mac, I wrote, My #1 Rule for Dating over 40: What's Yours? Mine was Be Yourself. I wasn't being sarcastic. I *would* be myself. If I ever dated when I was over forty. Then I listed Five ~~Philly~~ Restaurants Great for Dining Alone: Can *You* Dine Out Just One? I could not. I didn't even like sitting at the counter at the diner by myself. Even at the drive-through, I ordered two sodas. Then I tapped out a few more ideas.

Blog posts were the new potato chips. I couldn't write just one.

Darby's restaurant reviews and the Pop Philly archives served as invaluable resources. I made more lists of places to go and things to do even though I didn't have to go anywhere at all.

I perused the rest of the site. Graphics on every page boldly welcomed readers to share their own stories on *P-O-F.* On Holden's new *Nightclubs-to-Watch* page (*N-T-W*), a banner offered proof that life didn't end at thirty-nine. Thank God! Instead of letting the blog grow organically, Jade was forcing it the way Rachel forced amaryllis bulbs in February. Those bulbs grew into stalks sprouting vibrant, plate-size blossoms. Problem was, the flowers only lasted two weeks.

At eleven-thirty, the phone rang.

"What's up?" I said, after seeing Bruce's number.

"I guess Noah's sleeping?"

"He's been in bed for three hours." I wasn't giving an inch.

"You could call me, too, you know, before he goes to bed. Would that be so hard?"

"Would it be so hard to remember to call your son when he's awake?"

"I thought you were going to work with me, Iz."

"I am working with you. I'm trying to take care of Noah all the time and paying all the bills and working and trying to have a life. But, yes, you're right. I could have called you because Lord knows we wouldn't want Noah to think you had the idea yourself. I will call you tomorrow when we get home from school."

"I'll be out all day tomorrow, that's why I'm calling now."

"You said you wanted me to call, so I'll call. For Noah. Now you don't want me to call. Which is it?"

"Okay. Call my cell. I guess I can step out of a meeting for a few minutes."

Since Bruce wasn't working, I wasn't sure if "step out of a meeting" was California-speak for "step out of the ocean" or bay, or whatever. "When are you coming home? I mean, coming back? Your time is running out."

"Maybe next week for an interview. I've had two really promising phone interviews with this really great—"

"And when you're here, you'll take Noah for a few days."

"Jeez, Iz. If I can. I'm trying to get a job. I'm not sure what's so hard to understand."

What's so hard to understand is what I ever saw in Bruce in the first place.

I put the phone facedown on the sofa. I didn't have to talk to him unless it was in direct relation to Noah. And Noah was asleep. Bruce wasn't here. Bruce wasn't paying child support, scheduling a pickup time, or even apologizing. He was what? Calling to talk? To tell me he forgot to call?

I picked up the phone. "Let me know if you're going to be here. Don't just show up." I heard a loud whooshing sound, maybe the sea, or maybe Bruce was just holding up a giant shell to the phone to imitate a bad connection.

Then I sensed a presence and looked toward the stairs, where Noah stood in his Buzz Lightyear pajamas and pirate hat, eyes bright and wide as gold coins. I hadn't heard him pad down.

"Is that Daddy?"

Only for a moment did I consider saying no.

Just like every day, Donna busied herself at her station, setting out papers and a bucket of pencils, lining up sheets of green, white, and pink forms for the students to see. I enjoyed arriving early and talking to Donna; I hadn't done that for a month.

"How was your weekend? How's your mom doing? Remind me which class you're taking this semester?"

"It was nice. And she's well. Thanks for asking. Miss Lane, I have to tell you something. Dr. Howard has been looking for you in your office."

"Today?"

"Every morning for the past week or so. And he wants me to let him know when you arrive."

I looked at the clock. "It's eight o'clock, so please, tell him I'm here."

My day officially started at eight forty-five and my chairman wanted to know when I arrived? There couldn't be more layoffs. Could there? Not midyear. No. Anyway, I'd worked at Liberty longer than he had. I rarely took a lunch break, no matter when I walked through the door. I always took work home. I had always come to work *too early* for years. Now that I spent more time at home in the morning—or in the car in the parking lot logged on to Pop Philly on my phone—he was going to check up on me?

"Be careful, Miss Lane. There are rumblings about more layoffs."

Dr. Howard's office door opened. He was burly, but with soft features. Both were well matched to working with the kids at Liberty, where it was sometimes difficult, often challenging, always rewarding. Dr. Howard was also unapologetically old-fashioned and overdressed in a brown suit and wide burgundy tie.

"Nice to see you, Ms. Lane." Dr. Howard nodded, looked at the clock on the wall, then back to me. "Here early today, I see."

"Nice to see you, too." Where was the Phillies cap to hide behind when I really needed it?

Dr. Howard walked through our waiting area and disappeared among a few straggling students in the hall. He'd left me alone during his three years at Liberty. I knew the ropes, he said. Every time another counselor was let go, he assured me that I was the keeper. Maybe keepers came in forty-five minutes early.

"What time did Helen get here?"

"Around seven-thirty."

Maybe keepers arrive an hour early.

I left my office door open. I had no early appointments, no students waiting.

"So, how was *your* weekend?" Donna asked.

Was my office bugged? Was a hidden camera tucked into the

drop ceiling? I didn't want to talk about my weekend. I wanted to make sure I still had my job.

"It was fine," I said. "So happy to get back to work today, though!" I said it loud so the mic could pick up my enthusiasm. "What did *you* do?"

Donna rattled on as if Big Brother weren't part of the equation. "Now that Mom's okay, we took my parents out to dinner for their sixtieth wedding anniversary. I convinced my brothers and sisters to splurge. I mean, our parents aren't getting any younger, you know? Why not go all out? We went to Sebastian's."

I'd never been to Sebastian's, but according to Zagat, *Philadelphia* magazine, and Darby's review, it was one of the best new restaurants in the city.

Donna puttered at her computer, pressed buttons on the multi-line desk phone. "I don't usually read restaurant reviews, but I like the ones on Pop Philly. They're written by this young girl who doesn't seem affected, so it's all easy to understand, no fancy talk, you know what I mean?"

A chill rushed through me and I closed the door behind me, as if the phone in the door would start chiming at the mention of Pop Philly.

"That's your friend's Web site, right?"

"Uh-huh." When Jade launched Pop Philly, I handed out her business cards as if I were a proud papa handing out cigars.

Donna smiled excitedly. "Oh, there's a new blogger on there who writes all about being single and over forty. You should check it out. You would really like it, I bet. Today people are writing all about their best and worst Valentine's Days. It's verrry juicy."

Donna read *Philly over Forty.*

"What?"

"Oh, I know Valentine's Day isn't until next week, but everything's early these days, isn't it? Those heart-shaped boxes were on the shelves in ShopRite the week after Christmas. I should know because I bought one." Donna patted her nonexistent belly.

I must have gaped because she rushed out of her enclosed area and stood in front of me. She brushed invisible lint off my shoulders and then held them the way my mother did when she wanted to lecture me.

"I didn't mean that you needed to read a singles dating blog or that you care about Valentine's Day or candy or anything. I know the divorce must still be fresh for you. I obviously have no idea about your personal life, and anyway, since it's your BFF's Web site, you must read it every day."

My knees weakened. "Yes, I do."

I walked in ovals in my office, which was too narrow for walking in circles. Was my job in jeopardy? That was first. I couldn't deal with people I knew just mentioning *Philly over Forty* to me the way they mentioned bad weather. That was second. I mean, snow, sleet, rain, your anonymous blog, high winds. How on earth was I supposed to respond to that? I did a modified Lamaze breathing. Hoo hoo hoo. I sat in my chair but swiveled back and forth, back and forth, back and forth, until I was dizzy, then I picked up my cell phone which, then seemed to swivel without me.

"Donna's reading it," I said to Jade. *It* was code for *Philly over Forty*.

"Did you really think no one you knew was going to read it?"

"I knew people were going to read it. I like that people read it." I liked that the readers were involved and interested. I liked that my ideas and questions sparked conversations in the comments section. I just wanted it all to be from strangers that I would never meet in a bazillion years. Precisely. Bazillion.

"We had almost eight hundred thousand unique users last year, Pea. And it's growing every day. The average reader clicks on three pages or more, and on *P-O-F* alone, readers stay engaged for over three minutes. We know some of that is due to all those comments everyone is leaving, which is amazing. But if it makes you feel any better, thirty percent of the readers aren't even in Philly, although that's higher in the summer. You aren't going to be running into someone from Australia or Spain or even Pittsburgh anytime soon."

Oh, good. Now I was a global fraud.

"Donna just can't know it's me."

"Did she *say* she knew it was you?"

"No."

"Did she give you a look *implying* that she *thought* it *could* be you?"

"No."

"So it's a coincidence."

My heart rate slowed. I wasn't sure I believed in coincidences, but was that all this was? A chance mention of something public and popular? Maybe it wasn't coincidental, but inevitable, like saying I loved cheesesteaks and then thinking it's *so astonishing* that the person who just happened to be sitting next to me at Jim's Steaks loves cheesesteaks too.

"You're right," I said. "It just caught me off guard."

"Look, this is one person who read Darby's restaurant review of Sebastian's and happened to mention it to you, and one of the thousands who have read your Valentine's post so far who happened to mention it to you, by chance. You see Donna five days a week all day long. It isn't that unlikely, you know."

I wouldn't see Donna five days a week if I lost my job. But the idea of someone's knowing it was me, and me having to answer for the posts about Mac, and the insinuations that I was in a pretty damn good relationship and had a lot of insights into dating, gave me pause.

"And would it really be that bad to have some of the real people you're giving out advice to know who you are? Would it be so bad for Mac to know?"

I stood and walked in ovals again, shaking the hand that wasn't holding the phone. My mouth was dry. My skin was hot. "That wasn't the deal, remember? I don't want it public. I have Noah to think about. And Bruce. And my job. My job that I *care about and love so much and am so dedicated to.*"

"Why are you yelling?"

I cupped my mouth and whispered, "People are being laid off left and right in the district. I can't afford to be next. No one can know it's me, please." And you can't know I'm lying about Mac.

Steering the posts away from Mac and into the middle of reader traffic until I could ease out of this jam was much safer for everyone. I couldn't forget that I was helping Jade by writing this blog. She'd said so herself. She needed me. Jade had not needed me in a long time.

"I just thought you might want to take advantage of your popularity."

"How?"

"Drew had an idea. He thought maybe you and Mac could write something together. He's impressed with you, Pea. I like Drew, but he is *not* easy to impress."

"Call him off, J. Please. I can't."

"I want you to think about it, okay? But nobody is forcing you. You haven't written anything negative. I bet Mac would be flattered. Drew said he wished someone would write about him like that."

The Divorce Guru of Philadelphia was a hopeful romantic?

"What do you think I should say if Donna brings it up again? If she asks if I've read it yet."

"Tell her you think it's the best damn blog in the universe."

Only Jade could make me laugh when I felt nauseated. She'd done it in college after too much beer at Smokey Joe's, and she'd done it through my bouts of morning sickness.

"So, while I have you in a good mood, Pea, can you come over Wednesday night? I have the bloggers, designers, and other staffers coming for dinner. Just pizza, but we need to meet in person. You should be here. I need you to be here. And before you say anything, just bring Pirate Boy with you. I haven't seen my little buddy in weeks. I'll buy Pirate's Booty. That should make him happy. I see it in all the mom carts at Whole Foods."

"Noah loves Pirate's Booty!" Great, now the surveillance team would hear me talking about snack foods.

"See? I'm totally kid-friendly." Jade was totally Noah-friendly. "Pirate's Booty still sounds like a slutty Halloween costume to me, but what do I know?"

I guffawed and whispered, "Lots."

That night, Noah nestled next to me in bed. I stroked his hair as if keeping it in place. With a light touch I scratched his arm, knowing the rhythm would relax him, eventually send him into a deep sleep. I watched his torso rise and fall.

"Mommy, the other day Daddy said he's coming home soon."

"That's wonderful, honey. I know how much you miss him."

"Mommy?"

"Yes, Noah?"

"What's 'soon' mean?"

I was lying to my dearest friend, my closest cousin, my parents, brothers, and thousands of readers a day. But I would never lie to Noah.

"I don't know."

Noah deserved so much more than to contemplate the passage of time. And after all, *soon* was subjective. If I didn't understand how Bruce could leave Noah, certainly Noah didn't understand. Just by being born he had earned more than a faraway father and a makeshift home amid my memories. But did I?

Perhaps I wasn't meant to mother a houseful of children, but I was meant to be Noah's mother. I knew that from the moment that cherished stick had two pink lines. Noah was my *beshert,* my meant-to-be. My Jewish forefathers didn't mean it that way when they thought up the word, I knew that. It was Bruce whom they would have called my intended. And we *were* intended. For a time. Just not for forever.

With Noah asleep, I pulled away my hand and collected all the books. Pop-up pirate ships, flip-up pages, fuzzy lions to pet, and cardboard levers to pull. Noah had started reading on his own, part of his speech-therapy sessions at school. Sometimes I just wanted him to stay the way he was, stumbling over his *r*'s, in cutesy pajamas, wearing the eye patch that made everything so clear to us both.

Padding downstairs, I grabbed my laptop from the living room, my Phillies cap from the kitchen, and went back upstairs. I slipped in next to him and set the pillows as a wall between us and turned off the sound and turned down the brightness. He just snored, and it was all I wanted to hear.

I assumed people in all time zones and with all varieties of internal clocks were meeting on Facebook for the camaraderie I had on Pop Philly, the camaraderie I sought for my true self. But the pages stood still. Nothing new was on Rachel's profile, I didn't see any banter with Jeremy, and no matter how hard I tried, the inspirational quotes in colorful boxes did nothing to inspire me. And I couldn't talk to cute-cat videos; Felix would be jealous.

Maybe that was another thing about being married that I missed. Someone to talk to when everyone else was asleep. Although Bruce had been known to zonk out before the *Tonight* show, he was there. I could poke him with a "Hey, you know what?" and he'd open his eyes and pretend to listen. There had been a lot of pretending in our five-year marriage, but during the good times, which I tended to forget, there was also a lot of talking.

I knew hundreds of comments awaited on *Philly over Forty* but I hesitated. I yearned to banter with words that came out of my mouth and not my fingers. I wanted to talk and just be myself. Use my name. It was too late to call anyone, even Jade.

I opened the blog and scanned the page, ready to read comments at random, like a game. Click on page four, read comment fourteen. Click on page twenty-two, read two comments in a row. I was nothing if not creative. Just then, on page eleven, one comment jumped out with all capital letters.

YOU HAVEN'T WRITTEN ABOUT MAC IN DAYS. WELL, HE SEEMED TOO GOOD TO BE TRUE ANYWAY.—CD

My make-believe world had just gotten very real.

Chapter 14

Chinese Jump Rope

WEDNESDAY NIGHT I FOUND a parking spot on Bainbridge, only a half block from Jade's house. Noah seemed impervious to the cold. He clapped away breath clouds between his mittens during his gallop to the door.

Before Noah's finger touched the doorbell, Jade opened the door. She crouched and opened her arms, as if she'd been waiting all day for him to arrive. Noah flung himself at her. She looked up at me after opening her eyes, as if to say, *Thank you for sharing him with me.*

"Hi, handsome. Let me get a look at you."

She said that even when she'd seen him the day before. Taking Noah's hand, Jade stood and they walked inside. I stayed in the foyer for an extra second, as if by following I'd have interrupted something private.

When I closed the door behind me, Noah was already sitting on the kitchen counter collecting slices of apple from a tray.

"How about dinner?"

"This is just my first course, Mommy. Right, Aunt Jade?"

"Pizza won't be here for another forty-five minutes, and I knew little dude would be hungry." Jade lifted Noah down from the counter and transferred him to a chair at the kitchen table. Then she turned on a small flat-screen TV and Nickelodeon sprang to life.

"Thanks."

"No thanks necessary. He'll be fine for a while, right?"

Noah was eating an apple slice like an ear of corn. At this rate he'd be fine for an hour. "Sure."

"Great, everyone else will be here any minute."

The doorbell rang. No one was late for a meeting with Jade.

I waited on the sectional in Jade's office while Jade ushered in the Web-site troops. I stood, smiled, and nodded. Holden's two-handed handshake allowed me to relax. Our e-mail rapport was flourishing. I could ask him about the person who commented that Mac was too good to be true, but since there had been no repercussions, and no more mysterious comments, it wasn't an emergency. Even seeing Darby in her fitted sweater dress and tights reminded me that this was business, not just a hobby for her or Holden or any of the others I could have given birth to if I'd started at fifteen.

Andrew Mann walked in last, a graying head shorter than the sports blogger, Zach, who stood next to him. Jade smiled. She liked Coat Guy. Maybe more than she was willing to admit.

As the "kids" sat down on the sofa and the floor, pulling out tablets and laptops and talking in jargon, Jade crooked her finger at me. She laid her hand on Drew's back. The three of us walked to the great room.

"Have a seat," Jade said.

I chose the one lone overstuffed chair, as opposed to the ones that looked pretty but uncomfortable. Jade and Drew sat next to one another, half a cushion between them on the midcentury modern sofa. I only knew that it was midcentury modern because Jade had told me.

"Drew wants to talk to you about Mac."

My mouth fell open. Did Jade and Drew know? Was Drew the one commenting that Mac was too good to be true? Was it Jade? Was this her way of allowing me to confess so she didn't humiliate me completely? I would rather they just come out and say it, chastise me. Fire me.

"I'm sorry. Mac's not up for discussion."

"He needs to be," Jade said.

My pulse slowed.

Drew leaned closer, his elbows on his knees. "You've stopped writing about him. And those posts brought the most traffic. There's nothing to be embarrassed about. If I were Mac, I'd be flattered."

If you were Mac, you'd be invisible.

"You seem to be in a really good place with him. Why not let him know how much you appreciate things like when he put the glass in your screen door? Or how much you enjoyed just watching movies when Noah went to bed? I mean, I'm sure you tell him, but reading about it would boost his ego."

What did Andrew Mann know about needing an ego boost?

"I'm glad you like what I'm doing. Both of you. I really am.

But I can't have anyone knowing who I am on Pop Philly. Mac included." I had not yet addressed Drew by name. Did I call him Drew, or was that Jade's name for him? Andrew? Mr. Mann? It was the internal awkwardness of having *Coat Guy* on the tip of my tongue.

"I think people do know *exactly* who you are. They just don't know your name—Elizabeth Lane." Then Andrew Mann stood.

"Izzy."

"Excuse me?"

"You called me Elizabeth."

"Elizabeth is your name."

"Yes, but only one person calls me Elizabeth."

"Your mother?"

"No, my mother chose my nickname before I was born. I was named after my father's aunt." Why was I telling him something personal?

"Mac?"

"Excuse me?"

"Your boyfriend? The one we're talking about, the one you won't tell about *P-O-F,* the one who you're supposed to be writing about? Is he the one who calls you Elizabeth?"

"No!" They knew. They were waiting for me to crumble into a confession. But I wouldn't topple. My façade was sturdier than the truth. "I'm sorry."

"What are you sorry about exactly?" Jade asked.

I felt pushed and prodded and poked. "I don't know. I assume I'm doing something wrong or you wouldn't have pulled me aside here with Mr. Mann and then not said two words to me."

"Please don't call me Mr. Mann. That's my father. You can call me Drew. Or Andrew. Just don't call me Andy, because that's what my mother calls me." He smiled to match his bus-stop posters.

Charming was not going to get me to say more about Mac.

"Look," Andrew said, "we don't have a problem with the questions and the banter you're generating. People peruse dating information and online dating sites long before they get divorced. Like window-shopping before you need something. And sometimes couples going through divorce need to change lawyers."

"That's horrible!" I was cultivating a client base for a lawyer keen on spurring divorces. *I* was horrible.

"We just need to make sure you're still writing those posts about you and Mac and not just asking questions. The Mac posts spike traffic."

Jade nodded. "The psychology behind that is that the readers want relationship stories as much as or more than they want dating advice, but you've stopped talking about Mac. So we need a way for you to really get under the skin of your readers. If you're not going to do it with Mac, then we need you to spur some controversy."

"What if I don't have anything like that to say?"

"We're not asking you to lie," Drew said. "Just add a little attitude."

Too bad, because lying I could do.

"Would you excuse me for a second, ladies?" He headed down the hallway, presumably to the little Mann's room.

"What a jerk."

"He's a good guy, Pea. And he spends a lot of money advertising on the site. He made it possible for me to give you that check last month. And he'll be the one responsible for the check I give you next week. You know, the one that pays for Noah's day care?"

I wished Jade had told me who he was that night at Meema's. I didn't like feeling blindsided—by Jade, Mann, or irony. Or was it karma?

"Drew liked the concept of *Philly over Forty* and had a lot of money to spend. He's been a real friend to me, too. And he asked me for a favor."

Where was MBA Jade? Had her Web site been riding Mann's coattails for this past year? Did he dictate all the content? Did he own the restaurants with the five-star reviews?

Mann walked back toward us, and I stood, primed to rattle off the analytics on the key words that were bringing the biggest hits to *Philly over Forty,* how the traffic had remained steady since I'd stopped writing about Mac. Then he veered off toward the kitchen.

Jade and I watched as he sat in the chair next to Noah.

"What's going on in there?"

"Nothing. He likes kids."

"I'd like to know what they're talking about."

Then the doorbell buzzed; Noah yelled, "Pizza's here!"

As Jade and I stepped into the kitchen, Mann's phone buzzed. He typed in response. "I've got to go. Unexpected transportation emergency. Captain Noah, I hope you find that buried treasure."

"Arr," Noah said.

"Elizabeth, think about what I said. You're happy dating Mac, and obviously, Mac's a lucky guy. No reason he shouldn't know how lucky by learning about *P-O-F.*" Then he looked at Jade and lifted his eyebrows. I almost expected her to lean down and kiss him on the head.

After thirty minutes of statistics sharing, brainstorming, and pizza-eating with Jade's Pop Philly entourage, I couldn't stand it anymore. "I'm going to check on Noah."

"I'll go," Darby said.

"I'll go with you." Jade pointed at me and held out her hand like a crossing guard. Darby sat from her half-standing position.

In the kitchen, Jade handed Noah an ice cream sandwich while I replenished his construction paper.

"So what are you going to ask me that Mann couldn't stick around and ask me himself?"

"He's been through a lot. He's a good guy, Pea."

"How *good* exactly?"

She ignored my innuendo. Where was fun coconspirator Jade when I wanted her?

"Your posts are getting thousands of hits. He's impressed. He likes you. I can tell. If you weren't dating Mac . . . I'd fix you up."

Flabbergasted, I said nothing.

"What? That's a compliment. You do everything. And you're successful at everything. Working, parenting, and dating. I could not do all three and do them all well. That I know."

"Wait, Andrew Mann is single?"

"Yes, he's single. You didn't see a wedding ring, did you?"

I hadn't looked. "So I guess this means you and he really aren't . . ."

"Oh my God, no! We're just friends."

I was as relieved by her answer as I was flustered by her question. I didn't see how dating a divorce attorney could be a good idea for anyone.

"Oh, and one more thing. He desperately needs to get out of the office and out of the house. So, I promised I'd ask you. Just a casual dinner among friends."

I rolled my eyes, but smiled. I hadn't been out to dinner in a long time, and for Jade's sake, and my wallet's, I wanted to give Andrew Mann a chance.

"Great. It's about time anyway."

"About time for what?"

"For us to meet Mac."

Chapter 15

Musical Chairs

I ZIPPED MY PARKA, pulled on my hood, and walked two paces to Mrs. Feldman's house. Translucent snow covered the horse-and-buggy silhouette on the storm door, so I brushed it away, then cleared the frost on the glass. I knocked and waited, even though keys to Mrs. Feldman's doors were tucked in my coat pocket.

The front door opened much sooner than I expected, as if she had been anticipating my arrival. I heard the storm door unhitch.

"Elizabeth, what's wrong?"

"I just wanted to visit." I stood in the foyer but shut the door behind me, although the cold air had followed me inside.

"The children are coming for dinner." She pointed to the dining room. "Take off your coat, though, if you like."

Not the welcome I had expected. "It's nice that your family is coming for dinner." I stopped myself from asking why they were coming. Did there need to be a reason?

"It *is* nice," Mrs. Feldman said with a flat affect. "And I assume Noah is at a friend's house."

I nodded.

"That's nice, too."

"It is." It was nice because I hadn't had an afternoon or evening alone since Bruce took off for California. I worked at Liberty, picked up Noah, drove home, spent time with Noah, helped Noah with homework, cooked dinner, spent time with Noah, settled Noah into bed, and then wrote and read *Philly over Forty* and Pop Philly. And during all of that I was checking my messages and comments and statistics. I was also analyzing the wins and losses columns in my life—Ethan and Maya, win; my parents in Margate, win for them *and* for me; Bruce in California, loss; an extra check to cover expenses, win; lying to Jade, loss. Not spending time with Mrs. Feldman? Loss.

A plastic-covered tray layered with corned beef, roast beef, and turkey sat on the tableclothed dining-room table surrounded by bowls of tuna and potato salads, and coleslaw, as well as an array of mustard and mayonnaise packets—my condiment-OCD nightmare. There was just no way to avoid seepage and spillage with those things. My throat prickled. I also saw a stack of china plates, a huddle of cut-crystal water goblets, and a wooden box with a brass handle that I assumed held silverware. In my peripheral vision I saw Mrs. Feldman looking at me as I looked at the table. Her mouth was open, and the air lingered with her forgotten words. She wore a pressed apron, which I found strange considering the cold-cut menu. Maybe the apron had more to do with appearances than preparation, the way I'd kept on my work clothes instead of throwing on sweats before I came over, so that maybe, just maybe, I looked like I had somewhere to be.

Mrs. Feldman sat in the armchair at the head of her table. "What can I do for you, Elizabeth?"

The scent of briny kosher pickles filled my nose and made me queasy. "Is it a special occasion?"

"Absolutely not." Mrs. Feldman sounded curt and annoyed, as if I should have known the answer.

"Oh, I just thought . . . because of the china . . ."

"Well, if not now, when?"

I rubbed my hands together as if one idle moment had decreased their circulation. Without being asked, I lifted a few plates and set them around the table, evenly spaced. I finished with the plates and started on the goblets as Mrs. Feldman folded napkins into triangles, which seemed an uninspired choice, considering the Lenox, Waterford, and embroidered linen. Our rhythm seemed that of an old married couple, or maybe just lifetime friends. My lifetime.

"Jade wants to meet Mac," I said.

Mrs. Feldman continued folding. Corner to corner. Corner to corner. Then she ironed the seams with her thumb. I took the rest and placed them to the left of each plate, with deliberate sluggishness. I wanted instructions. A little to the right, Elizabeth. Straighten that one a bit. Is that a water spot on the tablespoon?

I shuffled to the left, remembering that sometimes Mrs. Feldman forgot and sometimes she didn't hear. I spoke louder. "Mac. You know, the man I made up for the blog posts I'm writing? For Jade's Web site? She wants to meet him."

"I know who you mean, Elizabeth. I'm not a nincompoop. I'm quite capable as a matter of fact. No one helped me get that china out of the cabinet or bring up the silver from the basement."

"I'm sorry, I just thought . . ." I stood, stunned.

"You thought I forgot because I'm old. Well, I am old, but I did not forget. I just have other things on my mind. Of course she wants to meet Mac. You're happy and he's the reason. I'm sure your cousin wants to meet him. I know he's not real and *I* want to meet him. It might be time for you to swallow your pride and tell the truth, Elizabeth."

Mrs. Feldman had never reprimanded me before. Not in thirty-nine years.

"If I were you, I'd take advantage of these few hours to yourself and think about what you've done by keeping this secret. Telling this lie. God, why are you here with me? You could take a bath, read a book, or even go out for a cocktail. Maybe you would meet someone." She patted her pile of napkins. "Someone real. Where do young people go around here anyway?"

Mrs. Feldman stood and put her hands on her hips as if this scenario was something she'd never considered before. Nor had I. Was there a place a divorced forty-year-old mom could go in the neighborhood to get a glass of wine? There was.

Next door in my kitchen.

"Really, dear. Don't you have something you'd rather be doing on a Friday night than waiting with your old neighbor for her family to arrive?" Her voice had softened but she lifted my coat from the banister and handed it to me.

"Are you angry with me?" This was not an easy question to ask because I had no idea of the answer.

She took my hand in hers with the touch of timid child. She was trembling. This had nothing to do with me.

"I think we should sit down," I said.

Mrs. Feldman nodded and I led her to the sofa and sat next to her, my coat on my lap. I didn't let go of her hand. "I'll leave when your family gets here, I promise." I patted her hand. "But I don't think you should be alone. You're not yourself."

"Oh, Elizabeth, who else could I be?"

I turned on all the lights in the room. Everything looked better in the light, or should have. What I saw was a deflated woman in her eighties, without the joie de vivre I'd come to enjoy, and admire. Mrs. Feldman settled back into the cushions on the sofa. Her shoulders eased as I lifted her legs onto a small footstool.

"What's wrong? You can tell me," I said. "I won't tell anyone if you don't want me to."

Mrs. Feldman had said that to me many times as I was growing up, usually during a game of Go Fish. As always, talking about something troublesome was easier when I was doing something unrelated, and when I wasn't looking at her, or anyone. We'd stare at the cards in our hands, plucking them and laying them down in the middle. Mrs. Feldman had been my confidant and sounding board when my parents were at the store, and sometimes when they were home. They had bequeathed me to her, and she'd taken me in, in every way. Once

I admitted I'd taken six dollars out of Eddie's wallet, and once I confessed I cut school and took the bus and the el into Center City with my girlfriends. I stared at my lap the time I'd told Mrs. Feldman I'd been rejected by Princeton and Brown, before I told my parents or even Ethan.

I stood and walked away, keeping my back to Mrs. Feldman. I rearranged the knickknacks on her shelves, but always moved them back into place. I had shifted four shelves worth of tchotchkes. I had eight to go.

"That's my wedding china in there. Did you know that?"

I did know. "Maybe I did know that, I'm not sure, maybe just remind me." If there was a nincompoop in the room, it was me, of that I was sure.

"It takes up a lot of space."

"That's what the china cabinet is for." I handled the little faux pirate chest, knowing how much Noah would like it, and I placed it back by the lineup of photo albums.

"It takes up a lot of space in my heart, too." I turned around to see Mrs. Feldman shaking her head, and my chest compressed with a stifled gasp. Her attachment to that china, to her napkins, to Good Street, was a testament to her life. "It reminds me of so many years growing up with my parents and grandparents and then a lifetime of holiday dinners with Sol and the boys.

"You should use it all the time, then. You don't need a special occasion to use good china." I needed to remember that.

"This could be the last time I ever use it."

I sat on the sofa. "Is everything okay?" I think I was trembling.

"At my age everything isn't okay, ever. But I try to be grateful for what I have, not focus on what I've lost. A little arthritis, but much less than many of friends. I don't see as good as I used to, but I'm not blind. And I know I forget things. But I don't forget feelings, Elizabeth. Or people. Or secrets."

She was still angry about Mac. I was sorry I'd ever saddled her with my secret—my lies—in the first place.

"I'm sorry I told you about Mac."

"Don't be sorry, dear. We all need someone we can trust."

"You can trust me." I'd brought her meals and cleaned her toilets and listened to her stories, but I'd never come right out and offered myself as a confidant. She deserved a grown-up friendship, not one of a little girl who needed care and companionship, although that was eerily similar to who I was now. "Tell me why this might be the last time you're going to be able to use your wedding china." I held my breath for a moment, then exhaled. The last thing Mrs. Feldman needed was for me to faint.

"They're going to pack up the china and move it to some storage unit."

"Who?"

"The children."

"Why?"

"They want me to sell."

"The china?" I clung to a remnant of hope.

"That's why they're all coming over tonight. To go through the boxes in the basement and take inventory. Pack up some things. That's what the boys have been talking about to me for months now in addition to my *farkakte* will. Selling the house. Moving."

"To where?" Mrs. Feldman could live anywhere—a senior community in the suburbs, Florida, Arizona. I didn't know about the other "boys," but Ray had money and he liked to use it. Flaunt it. His white Mercedes stuck out on Good Street like glitter on the side of a barn.

But Mrs. Feldman was subtle, serene, and embedded in Good Street like a bottle cap in wet cement. She was a fixture here for longer than I'd been alive, like the streetlamps and blistering sidewalk and cracks in the cement. She was as sturdy as the iron railings that led to our front doors, a character in the life story of everyone who had lived here. But maybe not anymore.

"It doesn't matter where, Elizabeth. It could be the Palace of Versailles. I don't want to go."

She looked at me with her blue eyes that back in the day must have made her a looker. I'd seen black-and-white photos of a young Mrs. Feldman, but none of her before she married.

I heard a knock at the door. I put my hand on Mrs. Feldman's shoulder. No matter how she and I were connected through strings of secrets that weaved through walls and across decades, we were not connected by blood or by law.

"Do you want me to talk to them?"

"No. It wouldn't do any good. They worry about me here, living alone, and I understand. I don't want to be any trouble. So if it eases their minds for me to be somewhere else, it's the least I can do."

"But you want to stay, right?"

"I need to stay."

Chapter 16
London Bridge

OUT OF THE CAR and into the bright sun and cold of a winter Saturday, I held Noah's mittened hand. I assured him that if had been twenty-two degrees at sea, pirates would have worn mittens, too.

"Remember what I told you?"

"I'm having a sleepover with Cousin Maya."

Noah had not yet questioned why Maya had no mommy, or why there weren't books full of photos of Maya as a baby, as there were for him. All he cared about was that Uncle Ethan and Maya were fun. That they loved him. That they were his family.

Noah and I swung our clasped hands back and forth. As we walked up Walnut Street and past Rittenhouse Square, I slowed our arms to quiet the memories. We arrived at Ethan's blue-painted front door, and the aroma of a wood-burning fire hung in the air like a canopy. The window boxes to our left were mounded with untouched snow. After the frost, they would overflow with impatiens, coleus, and ivy, meant to flourish in the shade of the honey locust, whose name I knew because of Ethan's neighborhood's effort to map its trees. I had a hard enough time mapping one day.

It was as if my brother had staged his front step for our benefit. More likely, for Maya's. Any other day I've have used my key, knocked, and walked in with a whistle or a childlike holler. But even now I wanted to respect this as Maya's house and assure her that her place didn't need to be earned, it needed to be assumed. Ethan had told me she sometimes had nightmares that she was alone. If Ethan and I had anything to do with it, Maya would never be alone.

Before Noah knocked, the door opened. There stood Maya, slight, yet sturdy in her stance. She was wearing jeans with lavender stitching that matched her lavender, long-sleeved T-shirt and the bow clipped above her ear. She looked as if she were dressed for school pictures.

"Hi, Maya! Noah's here for your sleepover!"

She smiled as she stepped back, making room for us to pass.

Ethan watched from the great room, his hands behind his back. He'd restored his eighteenth-century row house on the outside, but renovated on the inside, leaving original wood floors and an exposed brick wall as a nod to the past from his modern and minimalist lifestyle. Everything meshed. It always had. How was it that this little girl looked as if she belonged when she'd only just arrived?

"C'mon in, everybody," Ethan said. "And make sure the door is shut or the heat will escape."

Even with the chill, I warmed with Ethan's dad-words.

"Want to see my room?" Maya reached for Noah's hand. "It's purple now."

Noah looked at me, and I nodded. They held hands, Noah gripping the iron railing with the other as they stomped step by step up the steep flight and out of sight.

I turned to Ethan. "Oh. My. God. I want to eat her up."

He threw back his head and laughed. "You sound like Mom." In this case, it was a compliment.

I walked around the glass coffee table and noticed the fingerprints. I threw our coats at him and he tossed them over the back of a chaise that was already covered with a chenille blanket and about a dozen kid's books and the exact Barbie dolls Ethan swore he'd never buy for his daughter. I laughed.

"So, her room is purple now, huh?"

"Purple is the new pink."

We laughed.

I rifled through Ethan's fridge. "Give her real food, okay? An occasional Butterscotch Krimpet won't kill her." I knew that Ethan wasn't a glutton for healthiness, so to speak. He was my diner buddy, after all. But I also knew he'd want to do everything right. Just because Maya wasn't a newborn didn't mean this wasn't all new. "Tater Tots. I think kids need Tater Tots once a month." I made that up and fanned myself with the holiday issue of *Healthy Living* magazine. "Not turnip fries, you hear me?"

Ethan's arms were crossed in familiar humor and less frequent deference. "Well, your niece thinks canned green beans are a vegetable."

"When you're eight, canned green beans *are* a vegetable." And sometimes when you're thirty-nine.

Ethan walked over to me with open arms and embraced me in a brotherly bear hug. He whispered in my ear, "You're a really great mom, Iz."

How did he know what I needed to hear? I just shook my head. Ethan took my head in his hands and moved it up and down. "You're doing all the right things."

"I'm not." My voice cracked. We collapsed onto the sofa.

"I'll get you a drink." Ethan walked to the kitchen.

"It's eleven o'clock in the morning!"

Ethan waved a Ghirardelli cocoa canister in the air.

I should have known.

He topped our steaming mugs with square marshmallows that came out of a plastic box with VEGAN stamped on it. They were light and sweet, firm but soft, just like Ethan.

I thought of the elementary-school afternoons I spent at Mrs. Feldman's drinking Swiss Miss with tiny dried marshmallow bits.

"You need a plan," Ethan said.

"A plan for what?"

"For how to get out of this blogging gig and get rid of that Mac. And as far as this Andrew Mann goes, I think he's testing you."

"I think the universe is testing me."

"Do not be melodramatic. You did this to yourself."

"I did not. None of this would be happening if Bruce hadn't gone to California."

"Izzy. You started your other blog months ago and set the wheels in motion."

It was much more fun to blame Bruce.

With the kids fed and in front of a movie, Ethan and I banished ourselves to the enclosed porch at the back of the house. It was heated, but also warmed by the sun year-round.

"How about a plan for how you're going to wind—this—down, Madam Blogger." Ethan twirled his finger in the air, mimicking a funnel cloud from top to bottom.

I felt degrees of separation from my blogging persona. There was an ease to anonymity, freedom from reprisal—from others and myself. I could slough off snide remarks as being directed at *her,* not me. It was much like standing behind the fraying academic curtain at Liberty, where I helped the kids navigate their high school years with a point and a nudge, then launched them into the world, crossing my fingers and moving forward without them. There was counselor me. Now there was blogger me. There was mommy me. There was no-longer-wife me. I was on the rampant lookout for me-me.

"For now I need the money, E."

"Look, I'm only on call twice a month, but I'll pay you whatever Jade does and you take care of Maya those nights."

"You want me to be Maya's nanny?"

"No, I want you to be her aunt who pitches in to help your brother." He forced a smile that was both silly and serious.

"I'm not taking money to help you with Maya. But I work and I have Noah and now I have no Bruce to fall back on."

"Well, think about it. I cut back my hours since Maya arrived, but I have to get back to a regular schedule. So, I'll have to hire a stranger. To take care of my daughter. Your niece. A stranger! Oh my." Ethan's drama was accentuated by his rendition of Macaulay Culkin's *Home Alone* face.

"We're not crossing that line. I don't want to be Maya's babysitter, I want to be her aunt. So sometimes, yes, she can sleep over or come over to play or just hang out. Or if you have a date!"

"That's not going to happen for a while."

I didn't try to argue. I understood that dating wasn't his priority. Maybe someday it would be for both of us. Maybe not.

My phone buzzed and I answered. I didn't care who was calling.

"Hey, Rachel, what's up?"

"Nothing. Why does something have to be up?"

"It doesn't, but I'm at E's. Noah is spending the night."

"Oh, it's date night! I want to hear everything. Give Ethan my love and I'll talk to you later. Call me before you go out?"

I wish. "You bet."

I turned the phone facedown on the coffee table. "Rachel sends her love. You know she can't wait to get Maya with her girls again."

"I know. So what's up with her and Sir Jeremy?"

"Nothing that I know of."

"So does that mean you think there is something you don't know of?"

"I don't know. I don't want to think about it."

"That's always a good plan." Ethan was the family confronter and never let anything go. "I was thinking that while the kids are busy, maybe we could talk more about you."

"I'd rather talk about Maya."

"I know you would, but we have her whole life to talk about her." He ran his fingers through his hair that had no intention of thinning. "Let's look at this blog of yours together and figure out what's next, okay?" I was a helper. Ethan was a fixer. My fixer.

"Before you try to talk me out of it again, I need to tell you that I like it. I really like it. Is that bad?" I lifted my cell phone and clicked over to Pop Philly.

"Let's look at you on the big screen, okay? My baby sister in Retina Display!"

He pulled his seventeen-inch laptop from the end table. I preferred my vast online world and capped façade to be accessible only via smartphone or netbook monitor. I could handle anything I could shut off and put in my pocket. Or pocketbook.

"Let's see what's going on in the Land of Izzy Lane, shall we?" Mercifully, Ethan clicked right to my Valentine's Day post comments, where my photo was a thumbnail, not a portrait, where the readers were the focus, not me. "I liked the idea of this post. I might not like what you're doing, but you sure are doing it well."

I tamed a grin. I was doing it well. Readers were responding. And responding. And responding some more.

"People just really open up online. How did you know they would do that?"

"I didn't at first, but it happened with my old blog. People say things they'd never say in real life. Sometimes that's good; sometimes, not so much."

"Well, I'm serious. These people feel comfortable here, in

this space, with you. That's a testament to you, Iz, no matter if they know your name or not. You didn't become a counselor for no reason. You like to help people. And allowing people a safe place to vent is helping them. Why can't you do it as *you*?"

"I don't want anyone to know who I am. I'd be mortified! To have Bruce and, oh my God—Amber—reading personal things about me, no thank you. And everyone at work? Mom and Dad? Eddie wouldn't bother me so much, but Trish and her friends?"

"Jade and Rachel know it's you."

"Right, and they think I'm dating Mac. Like all of them!" I wiggled my index finger at the monitor's stream of comments.

"I don't want to collude with you here, but really, you don't even have to tell Jade or Andrew Mann anything. Just do it here, online. A few hundred people here have told you their worst and most humiliating Valentine's Days. Tell them yours. Although I have a feeling your worst is about to happen next week."

"Jeez. Thanks." But Ethan was right. What would be worse than having to fabricate things that didn't happen with someone who didn't exist?

I believed that the readers would handle the truth better than Jade. Certainly better than Andrew, who thought Mac would be flattered by what I'd written about him. Andrew and Jade and the Pop Philly cheerleading squad wanted a dating blog. They'd already dinged me for pulling back on the Mac stories. I had tried to get them to refocus and reinvent, but this was part of Jade's plan for Pop Philly. I wished she'd let me in on what exactly the plan was, but I guess I had no right to ask for that. If I told her there was no Mac, she'd have to go to Andrew and tell him there was no Mac. And then there would be no ads. Jade would lose money and possibly her business. And I'd lose Jade.

"It's not my birthday yet. That's when I promised."

Ethan was staring at the monitor, not paying attention to me. His mouth was moving as he read the comments. His eyebrows rose and furrowed, and he pursed his lips, mouthing a few silent *oohs*.

I read over his shoulder. The forgotten Valentine's Day. The regifted necklace. The chocolate-*flavored* candy. The drugstore flowers. The breakups. The worst stories were the ones where Valentine's Day had just been ignored. My heart tugged at the memory of my first Valentine's Day as a mom, when Bruce gave me a heart-shaped silver locket with Noah's photo inside, then ruined it by saying, "What choice did I have? If I didn't get you something nice, I'd be an asshole."

The best Valentine's Day stories listed diamond rings, puppies, breakfast in bed, and someone taking out the trash. One man wrote that his best Valentine's Day was when *he* received a stuffed animal and flowers. One woman wrote that her best Valentine's Day was when her husband had the flu. She didn't elaborate.

My eyes rested on a comment in all caps:

MAC SURE IS MIA. WOULD LOVE TO KNOW YOUR VALENTINE'S PLANS. I BET THEY'RE TOO GOOD TO BE TRUE.—CD

"Looks like someone's onto you, Iz."

Chapter 17

Tag

ETHAN WAS RIGHT. It had taken me the drive home to figure it out. I was being called out for a playground fight. What if others weren't so slow on the uptake? If CD's motives were obvious to Ethan, would someone else catch on, such as Jade? Or Andrew? What about Holden or Darby?

I took a deep breath and scanned the comments.

Don't complain.

How about some pictures?

Leave her alone.

What makes her an expert?

Go read a different blog.

What's with the hat?

I have a right to free speech.

People shouldn't be mean.

Any idiot could ask questions.

I like reading everyone's experiences.

How's the sex?

Stop being so serious, this is fun.

So where IS Mac anyway?

It's a blog not a therapist's office.

Where's her face?

Get a life!

The words moved on the page; the letters blurred with my thoughts. I looked away and inhaled a long, slow breath, focused on the good, the easy. Many of these people defended my stories, my right to privacy. Others screamed that being online meant I had no rights. Mostly people wavered. Didn't they always?

The Valentine's Day post had not only spurred readers to share their personal bests and worsts, but to look for mine. Didn't these people have anything better to do than dig into a harmless dalliance, a cop-out post, about stupid Valentine's Day? Where were the joyful, funny readers who kept me company late into the night? I'd thought about what they might want to know and what they might be feeling. I wanted to be who they wanted me to be. But who was that exactly?

I called Holden. I didn't care that it was Saturday evening. I didn't care that e-mail had been our only form of communication. If I called, he'd have to answer. (Didn't he?) And if I called, he couldn't forward our exchange to Jade or Darby.

I was nothing if not a visionary.

"So, you won't delete the comments?" It was more of an accusation than a question.

"No, that's what the readers want to see, and it's our policy not to delete anything that's not offensive." Holden's words were staccato, as if he were reading an instruction manual.

"Well, *I'm* offended."

"Sorry, but that doesn't count."

I heard muttering in the background. "I'm sorry I called, I'm sure you're busy." I wasn't sorry and didn't care.

"It's fine. Darby is just helping me paint my apartment."

Darby? Painting? I couldn't help picturing her in a dress, with combat boots, and a roller. I stopped myself. Who had time to decipher their relationship? Figuring out what to do next about CD was my priority. "And you can't track that CD person?"

"Well, I could. It would take a few days."

"And you can't stop this . . ."

"Troll?"

I had a blog troll—someone who popped up into a comments section just to start trouble that rippled through to the other readers and often created an online rebellion. I'd read about those. Someone who wouldn't even use her full name was sabotaging me. I coughed up the irony.

"I can start some tracking on Monday."

"Yes, please," I whispered, determined not to seem worried, but angry. "That would put my mind at ease. I mean, what if she's a psycho?"

"Well, more than likely she's just bored, and a little jealous of your popularity. Just keep doing your job. It's going really well."

"I can't concentrate with all this going on."

"Ignore it. Whatever you do, do not engage. Please. If it really becomes a problem, we can delete the posts, but right now this is sparking a lot of traffic."

"Right."

"We have a lawyer if there's danger. No one is threatening you, right?"

Technically, no.

"Look, some people are just troublemakers. Darby has this one guy . . ."

I heard more rumbling in the background.

"Darby had this one guy who disagreed with every review for the past year. If she said a restaurant was great, he said it was awful. If she said it was awful, he said it was great. And if a place was mediocre, well, he called that a cop-out. But it all started conversations about the restaurants and about Darby that lasted for days. That guy was always arguing with everyone."

"And that was a troll."

"That was an asshole."

Ethan and I agreed. I had to get rid of Mac. Had he been real, that would have been a sinister thought. But he wasn't. Yet even in the land of make believe, breaking up was hard to do.

~~Dear CD and other *Philly over Forty* Readers,~~

~~Dear Friends,~~

~~Dear Readers,~~

~~Hi, my friends.~~

Hi, friends.

I'm sorry that our Valentine's Day conversation has been overshadowed by questions about Mac. The truth is something I have been reluctant to share. Even with the personal nature of *Philly over Forty,* we all deserve privacy, don't you think?

Mac and I broke up.

I won't mention him again, but look forward to continuing to discuss dating perks and perils on *Philly over Forty.*

We're all in this together!

I hit SAVE DRAFT. It wouldn't be my next post, but this would be ready when I was ready. And then, without notice or reason, I missed him. Yes, I missed Mac, my imaginary boyfriend, as if the breakup were real. I actually missed the make-believe cockeyed grin and broad shoulders, his romantic gestures and perfect timing. I also missed the idea of creating it all, and of soothing my ego with my fictional beau. Mac had captured my attention and heart like my high school crush, Joe Donnelly. Joe didn't even know I existed, yet I'd planned our entire life together, down to the names of our children. Like Joe, Mac had been so special, so perfect—without really being, at all.

I'd moved on from Joe and now I'd move on from Mac. I knew two wrongs—inventing the boyfriend and then breaking up with him—didn't make a right, but it seemed as if two lies had woven together to make the truth. I was alone. I knew the place well and could navigate without secrets and lies.

With Valentine's Day looming, I knew Jade would call tomorrow to go over the week ahead. I didn't begrudge her business savvy or dedication, but I did begrudge her constant access to me. I e-mailed her because it was slower than a text but faster than a phone call. Sometimes I had to be my own superhero.

J,

Busy day.

Need some time off.

Talk to you Monday after work.

Love,

Pea

I called Rachel. "Sorry I didn't call earlier, it was a crazy day."

"Here, too." Rachel's voice was hoarse, her few words strained. "Look, I don't want to keep you. Is Mac there?"

"No, why?"

"Oh, I thought that was why Noah was sleeping at Ethan's."

"He's sleeping there to spend time with them." I was not up for a debate or discussion about Mac. "What's wrong?"

"Why does something have to be wrong?"

"It doesn't."

"I'm sure you're getting ready to go out, but I just wanted to see if you want to have dinner tomorrow. I'll come to you since it's a school night."

"Sure, the kids can have Souper Sunday like we used to."

"No kids."

Now I *knew* something was wrong.

Chapter 18

Halfball

It had been a day and a half since Mrs. Feldman's family had lumbered in, footsteps heavy with mandate. Had my next-door neighbor not divulged what was going on, I'd be lying on the sofa reading books with Noah, or building primary-colored dream houses out of plastic blocks while listening to him tell me every detail of his visit with Maya. But I knew where I was needed.

"We thought you might want some company," my dear boy announced, then looked up at me, eyes wide. "Did I say it right, Mommy?"

"Perfectly." Mrs. Feldman smiled. "And do you know what? I would like some company. Come in, come in."

Noah slipped off his coat and lifted the bucket of LEGOs out of my hands. He was as comfortable here as I had been as a child. As I was now. He would miss this, or likely, I would miss it on his behalf.

"You can build on the coffee table, Noah. My grandsons used to do that."

"I figured you had leftovers from Friday night, but if you need me to go to the supermarket, I'd be happy to."

"No need." Mrs. Feldman walked to the kitchen and I followed. She opened the fridge and pointed. "Mrs. Babayev brought me some *mastava*."

I raised my eyebrows.

"Soup. I think it has meat in it." She continued pointing to containers and wrinkle-silver-wrapped packages. "And Mr. Rodriguez brought me some tamales. Theresa Lombardi on the corner? She made me gravy—that's what she calls spaghetti sauce—and she also brought what she says are homemade raviolis, wrapped in that tinfoil there, but I peeked and they look like they're from ShopRite. Not that it matters. They must have seen the kids all coming in here the other night and thought I must be sick." Mrs. Feldman grunted. "Everyone brings food when you're sick, which is funny really, since when you're sick, you don't want to eat. Oh, and I have wonderful chocolate chip cookies from that skinny, young Miss Jackson who just moved in. I thought that was especially nice."

Mrs. Feldman picked out a few chocolate chip cookies, and as if called with a silent dinner bell, Noah appeared, LEGO sword in his hand.

"Don't make a mess." I sounded like my mother.

Mrs. Feldman looked at me, then back at Noah. "He won't make a mess, and if he does, it's not the end of the world, is it?"

"No."

"Oh, and I have something else for you." She reached under the sink and then handed Noah the tube from an empty paper-towel roll to add to his collection. Mrs. Feldman remembered everything.

With Noah back in the living room, I knew I had to ask my question or miss my chance. "Can I ask what happened Friday night?"

"You can." Mrs. Feldman was not going to make this easy. Nothing about this was easy.

"So, what happened?"

"They made their argument, and I made mine."

"And?"

"And, to the grandchildren, *assisted living* sounds luxurious. To the boys it sounds like a way to keep track of me—like the assistance is really for them, not for me. Although that's what they say. To me it just sounds like giving up."

Giving up was always the first step in the wrong direction. "So what did they say, exactly?"

"They say I'm too thin. Thin, schmin. I do the Silver Swimmer class at the JCC. And I've always been thin. I have my father's metabolism. But now they think I'm sickly. And see those magazines in the corner? I save them for the children, who need them for homework. No one orders magazines like they used to. But all of a sudden the boys say I'm neglecting things around here. One corner with a stack of papers and all of a sudden I'm a hoarder like on television. They want to know if someone is looking in on me, making sure I'm not leaving the stove on. You know . . . getting senile."

I opened my mouth and Mrs. Feldman put her hand on my arm. "You do a good job looking in on me, Elizabeth."

I hugged her.

Mrs. Feldman pulled back and turned away. "They want me to be safe. Live with people my own age." She tapped the table with both hands, as if trying to get my attention, which she already had. "What on earth makes them think I want to be around old people all the time? I have my friends at the JCC. I have my friends from Hadassah and the Sisterhood. That's enough old ladies for this old lady. I don't need bingo down the hall. I'll never have to leave the building. Any young people I'll meet are the ones who are there working. The only children I'll see are the ones that visit the other people—or when someone visits me. That's not the same as somebody building a town on my coffee table. Or skipping rope on my patio. Or even throwing a snowball at my window. And do you think someone at Shady Forest is going to make me tamales?" She tapped her temple three times with her forefinger as if joggling loose her thoughts. "And what if someone stops by looking for me?"

Who would look for Mrs. Feldman who didn't know where she'd gone? Some of her lady friends already lived in retirement villages or assisted-living communities. Others still lived with their husbands. Her friends, her family, her neighbors? We'd all know where she was.

"How about change-of-address cards?" Did people send those anymore? Mrs. Feldman could do that. Even if it took envelopes and stamps instead of e-cards and Excel spreadsheets. I could do that for her. I pictured an assembly line of me, Noah, and Mrs. Feldman stuffing and licking and stamping and addressing. "As for the memories, you take them with you." I'd think that would be the easy part.

"I couldn't take them all. The walls, the floors, the plates and spoons and cups. They all have memories attached to them. They make me remember."

"You'll take as much as you can. A cup, a plate, a book, a figurine. Better yet, I'll help you write down the things you don't want to forget, then you can just read them. We can get a journal, or a binder. It will be like a combination of an inventory and a memoir. Or we can do it on the computer. I'll bring my laptop over later and we can note everything you have. You can tell me stories about everything and I'll type them."

"And these would be just for me?"

"Yes, unless you wanted to share them with someone. Is there someone? I could make copies, or e-mail . . ."

"No." Mrs. Feldman gathered the waist of her blouse in her hands. "I'll keep my stories to myself. But thank you, Elizabeth." She smoothed the fabric she'd crumpled and looked at me as if she'd forgotten to say something or was searching for one particular word she couldn't find. Even I sometimes faltered for the right words. More than sometimes. So I waited.

"No matter what, we should make a list of everything you have," I said to break the silence. "Then if you're getting ready to move, you can look at the list and decide what to take. Do you know what the next step is?"

"If an apartment opens up, I'm next on the list. I'm pretty sure the boys paid for me to be at the top of that list. Chop-chop! They said you can't do that, but I didn't believe them."

I didn't either. Not sure what to say or do, I rose from the chair, shook some Ajax onto a sponge, and scrubbed the sink, which was already clean and dry.

"Come sit down, Elizabeth. I can't believe I'm saying this, but stop cleaning my sink."

I stopped and I sat.

"You're not planning to leave Good Street again, are you?"

"Not anytime soon." I had to remember why I was here. To have a life I could afford in a decent house in a decent neighborhood, not too far from work and near decent schools. I wondered if all I'd ever be able to hope for, strive toward, was "decent."

Mrs. Feldman walked into the living room and came back with the little pirate box. She handed it to me and I assumed she was bequeathing it to Noah. "Would you save this for me? I mean, not for me. But would you keep this once I've gone? Moved."

She opened the silverware drawer, reached into the back, and handed me a small bronze key. I was sure I could've opened the box with an uncurled paper clip, but I didn't want to dispel the myth that its contents were safe.

"Of course I will, but if this is so important, shouldn't you keep it?"

"It won't do me any good."

She handed me the box; it was the first time I'd felt its weight. "What exactly is in here?"

Mrs. Feldman raised her index finger to her lips as if to shush me. A lump formed in my throat and my thoughts ran amuck. I put the box on the table, picturing ashes, bones, drugs—none of which I really thought were inside, but my imagination had been in turbo drive lately. I said nothing. Mrs. Feldman said nothing. Noah stayed in the living room, engrossed in more LEGO building. Sometimes silence was more disturbing than a toddler banging on pots and pans.

"Don't worry, Elizabeth, if no one comes, just throw it away after I'm gone."

This time she didn't mean after she'd moved. "Who is going to come looking for this?"

"I'm not sure."

"When are they coming?"

"Probably never."

"Are you sure you need me to do this? Maybe you just need to keep the box." I pushed it across the table toward Mrs. Feldman, who pushed it back.

"No, please, keep it."

"What is in here?"

"A secret."

As much as I hated to admit it, I was growing frustrated with my friend, likely the way she felt about me and Mac. "What did you *do*?" I held up the box, unsure what I was touching.

"I put it in the box."

"Tell me what's in here."

Mrs. Feldman looked out the window. "It was easier to keep secrets back then. We didn't want to trouble anyone. We were embarrassed. Ashamed. Now it's the opposite. Today people tell the truth and take what's coming." She paused. "Like you'll do, Elizabeth."

Mrs. Feldman muttered a few more words, never looking

at me, or anywhere but out the window. I didn't know if this was a confession or a breakdown or a touch of dementia, or maybe all three. If this were Rachel or Jade, I'd have smacked them. Just to bring them back to reality. But no way was I going to slap Mrs. Feldman.

Instead, I grasped each of her hands tightly enough so that she turned and looked at me. "Mrs. Feldman, stop!"

She was still.

"Geraldine! Geraldine, look at me! Who is going to come for this box?"

"My daughter."

I let go of her hands. *My daughter.* Such simple words, but they might as well have been Mandarin or Swahili or Urdu.

I looked at this woman who'd been like a mother and grandmother to me, who was more maternal than my own mother, whose face filled my memory bank. I rifled through my mental files for a reference, a spark, a pinpointed moment where I would have my aha moment. Mrs. Feldman looked the same on the outside, but she'd flipped herself open to reveal another half. I could see it, empty. Her mouth curved into a frown, set deep with the lines of age and worry. And sadness.

"Where is she?" I asked.

"I don't know."

I insisted Mrs. Feldman come home with us. We sat together in the living room, and I prompted Noah with question after question about school, LEGOs, pirates, and Maya—anything I could think of, so the conversation stayed focused on him.

Then I offered Mrs. Feldman books, magazines, and the remote control while I went upstairs for Noah's bedtime rituals. I needed to spend time with him, end the day on a note of normalcy. For both of us.

Back downstairs, I didn't know where to begin. I reclined in my dad's chair to feign nonchalance. Was it my job to coax this information out of her? If she wanted me to be her secret's keeper, perhaps she should have been prepared to tell me everything. My head throbbed, as if my brain were full and I needed to upgrade its software. I needed more space for all the secrets. Mine, Mrs. Feldman's, and even Rachel's. Rachel, who would be here later.

"Secrets get under your skin," Mrs. Feldman said without looking at me. "They become so much a part of you they become invisible—to your head, to your heart—because they have to be. It's the only way to protect yourself."

Enough with the mumbo jumbo. "Where's your daughter?"

"I don't know."

"Is she alive?" I wondered if this was a resurgence of grief, a moment in which Mrs. Feldman had forgotten what year it was, and that she'd mourned a child decades ago.

"Honestly, I don't know. I gave her away. I was fifteen when I had her."

I sat up and the recliner snapped to attention. My insides ached. My hands held my stomach, which twanged with a phantom flutter. "I'm so sorry."

We sat in silence, my comfort unbalanced. An empty, almost-hungry feeling passed through me.

"I know what it's like to lose a baby." I had never said that aloud before. I didn't really know, I only sort of knew. A pregnancy had prompted Bruce and me to marry. "I had a miscarriage right after Bruce and I got married. I wanted that baby so badly. I always knew I wanted kids, and then I got pregnant and felt like my world was wrapped with a big bow." I remembered shopping for maternity clothes, wedding invitations, honeymoon trips, cribs . . .

"I know," Mrs. Feldman said.

"No one knew. Ever."

"I knew you were pregnant at your wedding, and I knew you weren't pregnant the next time I saw you."

"You never said anything."

"Of course not. That secret was yours to keep. As was mine."

"So why tell me now?" It was flattering to be trusted, but also encumbering.

"I'm tired. Tired of wondering if one day the baby I gave away when I was just a baby myself will show up looking for me. Or maybe her children. Or her grandchildren. But if I'm not here . . ." Mrs. Feldman's voice caught in her throat.

"Did you want to keep the baby?"

"That wasn't an option, dear. It was 1944. This was a *shanda,* a disgrace to my parents, and to me, and to anyone in my family who knew. A nice Jewish girl getting pregnant? Let alone by an Italian boy whose father made pizzas and whose uncles were priests?" It wasn't sinister at all. It was young love. "They found out about the baby and Tony, and in two shakes my parents drove me to Staten Island. But this was not a trip to summer camp." Mrs. Feldman shook her index finger back and forth like a metronome. "No, no, no. This was the Lakeview Home for

Jewish Unwed Mothers. When I got home seven months later, my parents and half my family had moved from South Philly to the Northeast. They might as well have moved us to the moon. I wasn't ever going to see my old friends again. No one mentioned the baby ever again. I never saw Tony again. Ever. The talk of the family that summer was that I was going into the eleventh grade when school started again. I was a grade ahead. One thing about pregnant Jewish girls, they brought in the best tutors for us."

"And then?"

"And then nothing. I graduated from high school. I worked at Gimbels. I met Sol. I got married. I was supposed to forget. Not just 'not mention it'—but really forget. No one went to a therapist in those days. There were no support groups. Behind my parents' back I wrote a letter to one of the very nice nurses at Lakeview. I begged her to put our new address in my baby's file. I put three silver dollars I'd gotten as birthday presents from my nana over the years into the envelope as a bribe, or I thought that maybe, if the nurse was very nice, she would put them in the file and one day my daughter would know I cared about her. I just knew that if my daughter ever wanted to meet me, the records would likely only have my parents' South Philly address or a phony address. How would she find me? I don't know if my daughter ever looked for me, or if that nurse ever even received the letter."

"You never tried to contact that nurse again?"

"No. It wasn't like now. No tap, tap, click, click. And honestly, Elizabeth, I owed it to Sol to be a good wife and to the boys to be a good mother."

"And you were." I had no idea what kind of a wife or mother Mrs. Feldman had been, only what I'd assumed based on our relationship. I was beginning to think I didn't know Geraldine Feldman at all.

"But Mr. Feldman must have wanted to help you find her, and your sons must have the means to dig through whatever red tape there is to get some answers. Things are different now. You know that. You could have started looking years ago."

"Elizabeth, when I said it was a secret, I meant it. The boys don't know about the baby. None of my friends know about the baby." Mrs. Feldman sighed in a tone filled with regret, not joyfulness. "She'd be seventy now and I still think of her as a baby. Sol didn't know about her either. I lied to him for our entire marriage."

I bit my bottom lip. She'd never told her husband. Every time someone asked how many children she'd had, she'd said three when the answer was four. Every time there'd been a conversation about mothers and daughters, Mrs. Feldman tucked back the secret a little further, perpetuating the lie.

My angst about Mac, Pop Philly, and Jade were blips compared to what Mrs. Feldman had gone through. What she was still going through after seventy years. Her trust was a gift. As was my newfound perspective.

"I will do whatever you need me to do," I said.

Mrs. Feldman had relaxed into the sofa cushions, and it made her appear pliant and frail. "Thank you, dear. I know it's a lot to ask. I know it was a lot to hear."

I thought of all the hours playing with paper dolls, eating cookies, steeping tea, talking, dusting tchotchkes, and folding napkins. "It's nothing." And it was nothing. Nothing compared to the manicured and delicate, yet strong, maternal hand she offered throughout my childhood, and still. "But it might help if I knew her name. Do you know what her adoptive family named her?"

"I don't know anything about her except for her birthday, of course, and the name on her birth certificate. I'm sure her new family changed it. She probably doesn't know her real name. Her beautiful name." Mrs. Feldman touched her lips as if to keep it inside.

I knew what she was going to say next. I just nodded and she nodded back. Our bond had always been strong, sealed the day my parents brought me home to Good Street from Rolling Hill Hospital. I asked the question even though I knew the answer.

"What did you name her?"

Mrs. Feldman smiled and told the rest of her secret. "I called her Elizabeth."

Chapter 19

Tensies

I SAT ON THE floor by Noah's bed, my head against the side of his mattress. His wispy breathing sounded like a baby's. His eyelids still fluttered as he slept, and I imagined he watched swashbuckling adventures unfold before him. I brushed the plush royal-blue carpet with my palm, knowing that with each stroke, the hue changed even though I couldn't see it. There was so much going on I couldn't see. I knew that now more than ever before. Mrs. Feldman had a daughter. Rachel was avoiding me. She hadn't shown up tonight, hadn't answered texts, and my calls went straight to voice mail. She *had* updated her Facebook status with vague annotations of busyness and joy. Why weren't people just busy and joyful instead of busy and joyful and sharing it with the world?

Noah shifted on the bed, and his foot pushed out from his blankets and dangled in front of my face. As I slid his foot back to warmth and coziness, my disparate thoughts came together.

I claimed I'd moved back to Good Street because of what I'd lost and labeled it an act of surrender. I thought nothing could be as good as the life I'd planned with Bruce, so why even bother? But perhaps my divorce was not a defeat. Perhaps it was a challenge. *To be better. Do better. Have better.* Perhaps I'd moved back to Good Street not because of what I'd lost, but because of what I *had*. Mrs. Feldman. Familiarity. Memories. A house that was already a home. Maybe what I *had* was the chutzpah to make it on my own. The comfort and safety of this house, this street, this life, didn't have to be cop-outs, they could be catalysts.

I tiptoed out of Noah's room and into mine. Mrs. Feldman's box was on my nightstand. The box needed safekeeping away from a little pirate's prying eyes and hopeful hands.

In the living room I sat on the sofa with my laptop, and Googled *Lakeview Home for Jewish Unwed Mothers*. I found one message board with a half dozen men and women looking for birth mothers. None of the information corresponded with Mrs. Feldman's. It was not my job to look for her Elizabeth, or whatever this woman's name was now. I repeated this inside my head. It was just my job to hold on to the box, to hand it over if someone came looking for it.

But do people look for treasures they don't know exist? Even pirates follow maps.

For now I tucked Mrs. Feldman's secret into the bread drawer with my Phillies cap and pushed both aside in my thoughts as my cell phone lit up with Rachel's face and ringtone.

"Hey."

"I'm sorry. Seth and I started talking . . . it just wasn't the right time to leave."

"Okay."

"How about I bring dinner tomorrow? Just a quick one with the kids? At your house after work?"

"I've heard that before."

"No, really, Iz. I need to talk to you in person."

"Are you okay?"

"Yes, of course I'm okay. Actually, I'm better than okay."

Rachel made me dizzy. "I'm always here for you, Rache. But you have to show up."

"Oh my God, Iz. Let it go. I get it. You're *busy*."

I imagined Rachel rolling her eyes. Yes, I was busy. Busy envisioning my cousin snapping seductive selfies and posting them on Facebook. Busy worrying I was tarnishing my best friend's business. I was also busy juggling students and parents and paperwork at Liberty. And I was busy trying to ignore Mrs. Feldman's secret.

The next day I didn't emerge from my office until lunchtime, avoiding any impromptu encounters with Dr. Howard. Since Donna's warning, I'd arrived by eight- fifteen at the latest, although Helen always seemed to be on her second cup of office coffee by then.

Today, for four and a half hours, a parade of graduating seniors marched into my office needing help with FAFSA, college applications, recommendations, and graduation requirements. One freshman, three juniors, and a sophomore handed in both real and fabricated paperwork proving they lived in the district. And a Ukrainian translator waited for the arrival of the

Tkachenko family so that Dennis Tkachenko's parents, grandparents, aunts, and uncles could discuss his college options.

Still, I needed sustenance and a change of scenery, just for five minutes. Without looking into the waiting room or toward Dr. Howard's door, I hurried to the empty office that used to belong to another counselor, a bagel with cream cheese clutched in one hand, a Styrofoam cup in the other. The door was ajar so I tapped it with my hip and flipped on the light with my elbow.

"Hi, Miss. Lane."

I flinched and water spilled as I set down the cup. "Donna, why are you in here? I mean, why are you in here in the dark?"

"Sorry, I just had to answer a quick personal phone call. I didn't think I'd get the chance to take a real lunch break today, so I brought my lunch in here." Donna's face drooped, and her eyes widened. I hadn't meant to reprimand her, yet I had. I noticed her lit cell phone and a half-eaten cardboard-box lasagna.

"Eat, talk." I waved my hand as if shooing her away. "I'll go back to my office." I peeked back out into the waiting room I'd sneaked past. Every chair was filled except the broken ones. Kids' heads hung to their chests, fingers twiddled, pencils twirled.

"Thank you." Donna typed on her phone as she talked to me.

"Is everything okay?"

"It's my mother—" Donna didn't look up.

I cringed. That morning I'd waved at Donna as I beelined to my office, still buzzing from Mrs. Feldman's news and Rachel's abandonment. I hadn't even poked out to say hello or to ask about Donna's weekend. "Do you need to go home?"

"It's her hip. She'll be fine. But thank you for asking."

"Please give her my best."

"Do you mind if I sit here for a minute? I just need to catch my breath before I go back out there. Organizing those students while I'm dealing with the doctors and my sisters is not easy. They don't always understand what I do, and that I can't always talk."

I could relate. "Of course you can stay here. Do you mind some company?"

Before Donna could answer, I unwrapped my bagel. Donna said nothing. She just stared at her phone. Scrolled with her index finger. Shook her head. Scrolled some more.

"Is everything else okay with your mom?"

"Oh, I'm sorry, yes. She'll be fine. She's tough."

"Oh, I just thought . . ."

Donna held up her phone. "This?" She tapped the screen and turned it to me. "My guilty pleasure." *Philly over Forty*. "Not that I haven't tried not to be single, but since I am . . ." She laughed louder than she should have. "Nothing new on here today, though. Which is strange."

Nothing new on *Philly over Forty,* that was absurd. It was Monday. My weekend flashed though my mind. All those comments on my Valentine's Day post, written in anticipation—in fear—of "the big day." Then there was CD. Ethan and Maya. Mrs. Feldman and Elizabeth. Rachel and . . . Oh, no. I forgot to upload my Monday post. No, I forgot to *write* my Monday post! And I could do nothing about it until tonight.

I stopped chewing and just swallowed. The bagel clump lodged in my throat. I reached for my cup and forced down my bite with a swig of water.

"You look pale, Miss. Lane. Do you need the Pepto?"

Donna was a devotee of placing a definite article before a proper noun, as was my mother, who always shopped at *the Ac-a-me* when I was growing up. I took classes at Penn to rid myself not only of the Northeast Philly burr, but its syntax. Yet Donna's colloquialism warmed me. Comfort lurked deep within its renounced familiarity.

And, yes, at this moment, *the Pepto* was just what I needed.

I sat in my car in the parking lot outside the JCC, where Noah attended his after-school program. Where I'd paid this month's bill on my own. Jade hadn't even tried to contact me, and she was always the one who blinked first.

Ripe with apprehension, I called her.

"Hello?"

"I'm sorry." That apology had more layers than she knew.

"Are you okay?"

"Uh-huh."

"I was worried about you, but I didn't want to bother you, considering."

"Considering what?" Was something wrong with Noah? With Bruce out of town, Jade's third emergency contact rank had been bumped to second.

"I know about Mac, Pea."

The Pepto crept to the back of my throat. "I'm so sorry, I should have told you, it wasn't right, but I didn't know what else to do. I promise I'll make it up to you." I held the steering wheel so tight my hand cramped. This was finally over. The bad, the good, the lying.

"Make it up to me? I should be making it up to you. My best friend breaks up with her boyfriend and doesn't tell me? You think *Philly over Forty* is more important than you are?"

"What are you talking about?" Now five minutes had passed and I had to get Noah or pay overtime. I left my car, cell to my ear, and walked through the parking lot. "I honestly have no idea."

"When you didn't post today, Holden checked your drafts. Pea, you should have told me you broke up with Mac."

Oh my God. My breakup post! Holden had accessed it. Of course he had. When there was no new post by nine this morning, he tapped and snapped and wiggled his nose and saw my draft.

"There's more to it. But I'm picking up Noah now."

"Of course there's more to it. We can talk about it Friday night." I walked through the JCC doors and smiled at the parents and kids leaving the building. "Pea? Friday night? Dinner? You, me, Andrew?"

"Right."

"Look, I'm sorry about this, but it will all work out. For you and for us. Do you want Holden to publish the post?"

If I let Holden push the magic PUBLISH button, my troubles would end. Although new ones would likely begin.

"No! Don't publish it. It's not what you think."

"You'd be surprised what I'm thinking, Pea."

Maybe not.

— Chapter 20 —

Monkey in the Middle

RACHEL ARRIVED WITH FOUR kids and two pizzas. We settled all the kids in the kitchen and ourselves in the living room.

"Sit with me," Rachel said, patting my sofa.

Had Jade told her I'd broken up with Mac?

"I have to tell you something," she said.

This wasn't about me at all.

"I met Jeremy for coffee."

"Okay," I said softly and evenly, while my heart rate increased. "What does that mean, exactly?"

"It means having coffee!" Rachel twirled a curl near her ear with one finger, her eyes cast toward the front window. "I don't know what to do."

"What happened?"

"Nothing. But I wanted something to happen."

"Wanting is different from doing. But you're sure nothing happened?"

Rachel nodded. "I'm sure. But does that matter?"

"Of course it matters."

"I'm not sure how to stop."

"No more Facebook photos. No more talking or texting. If you have to see him, you better have a lot of other people around. Whatever's wrong, this isn't going to help you fix it."

The past had wriggled through a crack in the universe called the Internet and landed where it didn't belong. In the present.

"It was so easy. So fun. So innocent. Until it wasn't."

I did not want details. "I understand." Rachel was right. It *was* easy and innocent when everything was contained online—or it seemed so—but then the online life seeped into real life.

She sat up, looked at me, and waited. "What did you do?"

"What do you mean?"

"You said you understand. *What did you do?*"

It was now or never. Plus, telling her would alleviate some of her guilt. Not all of it, I hoped, but some.

"I made Mac up. To Bruce, on my blog, to you, to Jade, to everyone."

"Yes, I know. His name's not Mac. At this point I'm figuring I'll never know his real name—"

"No, listen to me. I haven't been on a date in months."

"Sure you have. Just last week—"

"I didn't. I lied."

"Where *did* you go?"

"No, pay attention. There was never any Mac."

"So you didn't break up?"

"No! There was no one to break up with!" Jade *had* told her about the breakup. Could this get any more complicated? Stupid question. Of course it could.

"So you never really dated this guy who's name isn't Mac?"

This version of Who's on First wasn't funny. "He's imaginary, Rache." Then I knew how to make her understand. The only thing that held no ambiguity. "Mac is like Tiny Maggie."

I watched as realization settled over her. I watched as her chin dropped; her mouth opened as wide as it could. Tiny Maggie was Rachel's one-inch-tall, blond-haired, blue-eyed imaginary friend who lived under her bed in a shoebox and slept on a bed made of dominoes until Rachel was six.

I said nothing and cupped my hand, the way Rachel insisted upon every time she'd "handed me" Tiny Maggie.

"Wow." It wasn't the good kind of *wow.* "I need a minute to wrap my head around this. I was so *happy* for you. And you know, Jade's really worried about you."

I felt smaller than Tiny Maggie.

We chased the kids from the kitchen, but didn't clean the dishes or wrap the leftovers. Instead, I stared out the window and talked, while Rachel listened. Then I sat at the table. Rachel talked and I listened. It was past everyone's bedtime when we were finished.

"We're a mess," she said.

And now it was time to clean up.

I buckled myself into the passenger seat of Jade's BMW, while looking up at my living-room window. Inside, Darby corralled Valentine's-candy-charged Noah. My guilt was assuaged by heated leather seats.

"They'll be fine," Jade said. "It's like a mutual admiration society in there."

"What's up with that?"

"That kid of yours is pretty great."

"That's not what I meant and you know it."

"Darby has a bunch of younger brothers and sisters. I think she's just one of those kid people. Like you. She reminds me of you, actually."

I shuddered. The few times I'd been in Darby's company, I'd felt picked on, even bullied, and even in my own home. Noah seemed to think she was okay. Plus, Darby was babysitting on Valentine's Day, simply at the request of Jade. I wondered how Holden felt about that.

"Where are we going?" I did not want to be in a restaurant with candlelight and tablecloths, even with Jade. I'd have suggested a drive-through, but my best friend had her standards.

"Why doesn't Andrew have plans on Valentine's Day?"

"Why don't you ask him?"

"No thanks."

"Forget about the faux holiday. I did. I figured we'd go to the Oxford Diner—is that okay? We're going to keep your mind off you-know-who, and that seems like one of the few places that won't be dripping in hearts and roses."

"Thanks." The Oxford would help me forget about Valentine's Day and my fake breakup with fake Mac. I'd focus on Jade, her and Andrew's plans for Pop Philly, and how I figured into them.

But the parking lot was empty. The diner was dark. Jade parked by the steps and I ran to the front door: CLOSED DUE TO PARTIAL ELECTRICAL OUTAGE. Closed? Diners didn't close. Diners stayed open twenty-four hours a day, seven days a week. Didn't a closed diner violate the diner code of ethics?

"There has to be somewhere else to eat around here that won't be crowded or expensive or junk food," Jade said as I slammed the car door.

"Sure." I yanked off my gloves. I pointed to the neon signs that lined the street ahead of us.

"Not a chain restaurant."

"Can't help you. I'm the mother of a five-year-old."

An SUV pulled up alongside Jade. *The diner's closed,* Jade mouthed.

Andrew Mann looked over and motioned as if to say, *Follow me.*

Within minutes I was hanging up my coat in a different diner, one I hadn't been in since high school. This place had not been renovated, and I remembered the amber glass and globe lights as if I'd been here yesterday.

Andrew slid into the booth and scooted toward the wall. I did the same on the opposite side. Jade sat next to me and fiddled with the bangles on her wrist. The jingling got on my nerves as if it were a leaky faucet.

"How do you know about this place?" I asked.

"I grew up here."

I looked up from my menu and at Andrew. When seated, he seemed to be my height. "Where?"

"Right down the street."

"You grew up here?"

"Yes, that's what I said."

The kids from this neighborhood attended a different high school from my brothers and me, but many belonged to our synagogue, and some had worked in my parents' store. "Did you know Howie Solomon or the Kahn kids?"

"I was the best man at Howie and Lisa's wedding. How did you know him?"

"Howie worked for my parents. And I went to camp with Lisa."

"Wait. You're a *Lane Hardware* Lane?"

I nodded. He knew our store? Everyone did. But had Andrew come into the store any of the summers I'd worked there? Even through high school, anyone—even a guy around my age—buying a screwdriver or a gallon of paint had seemed the same to me: boring. I plucked a napkin from the metal dispenser, unfolded the rectangle, and smoothed the creases. Andrew knew Howie and Lisa. Howie was older than me, but younger than my brothers. Lisa had grown up in Cheltenham, but went to Camp America with me for eight years. My parents had attended that wedding. As a twenty-nine-year-old, single woman invited without a date, and without the desire for a wedding-night hookup, I had declined.

"You know Howie and Lisa. How about that!"

"You know Howie and Lisa so I can't know them?"

"No . . . I just didn't think . . ."

Andrew looked at his menu. "Exactly. Just think. We might have met a long time ago. Even at the wedding. We could have been old friends by now. Funny how we've never crossed paths."

"Hey, this is business, you can play Jewish geography later, okay? If we don't talk business, I can't write this off."

"Sorry," I said. "No Valentine's Day plans, Andrew?"

"Stop!" Jade said.

"I write a dating blog, it's Valentine's Day—that's business if you ask me."

"I'm here with you two, so I guess these are my plans," Andrew said. "I could do worse."

Jade's leg swept past mine and kicked Andrew under the table. "You're very funny."

"Okay, I confess. My Valentine's Day plans were over before dinner. Thank you for asking. What about you? Why aren't you with Mac?"

Damn.

Jade put her hand on my arm. "Without going into any details, Drew, there is no more Mac."

"I figured."

"What do you mean you figured?" I really had to move this conversation in another direction. "Where's our waitress? I'm starving."

"These matzo balls are perfect. Just the right balance of lightness and lead." I chuckled at my own joke.

I had talked about my soup, Andrew's Reuben, Jade's Cobb salad, and the waitresses' retro black-and-white uniforms that I knew weren't meant to be retro. Andrew popped the last bite of his sandwich into his mouth, followed by a french-fry chaser. I kept my hands away from the ketchup bottle, although I noticed that when Andrew poured, a few drops landed in the lid.

"Well, speaking of perfect, that Mac was too perfect, if you ask me. Not my type."

I raised my eyebrows.

"No, not that. I just mean that perfect guys make guys like me look bad."

"Oh, is that your problem?"

"Be nice," Jade said. "We are here to talk business!"

"Fine. Talk business."

"Drew and I were discussing a new direction for *P-O-F.* . . ."

"I don't think that's going to work for me, unless by 'new direction' you mean no dating."

"You don't even know what the direction is!" Andrew shook his head.

"We're going big, Pea. I can't give you all the details, but we're launching sites in new markets, and we want you to be on each one!"

All of a sudden I realized my soup was cold, or maybe if was my body. "I can't do any more than I'm doing. I have tons of work at Liberty, and basically I'm Noah's only parent, and it doesn't really seem right to blog about dating when I'm not dating." That was the most honest I'd been.

"I don't necessarily agree with that, but still, this is different. Remember Dear Abby?"

"Yes . . ."

"We want you to be *our* Dear Abby. You can take questions from anywhere, and the column will be on all our sites. What do you think?"

"Isn't Dear Abby copyrighted or something?" I said.

"Not that you'd actually be Dear Abby, just like Dear Abby. Dear Izzy! We'll target singles over forty, but it won't just be about dating. Maybe someone will ask about parenting or travel or buying a house. We'll call in experts, too, but it's *your* column. Not much different than what you're doing now, but the focus is not on you. We figured that's what you'd want, right? No more trolls!" Jade put her arm around me and squeezed twice.

Her words jumbled in my brain with each one. "Who's *we*?"

"Drew and me."

"So, you—and Andrew—who doesn't know me at all—no offense—made this decision on my behalf? I have had enough of someone else deciding what was right for me." I glared at Jade. "*Dear Izzy*? Are you telling me I can't do this if I'm not willing to use my real name?"

"No, no, we're asking. *I'm* asking. I want you to be part of this for the long haul, Pea. You don't know when Bruce is coming back. You don't want to rely on him anyway. This will be an extra paycheck. Just like now. Maybe even more in the future."

"I'm not using my real name."

"Think about it this way," Andrew said. "You're good at what you do. You can still use fake names for any man you might meet. Like—if *we* went out, you could call me Hercules, for instance."

Jade laughed. She was so predictable.

"You're kidding, right?" I didn't care which of them answered.

"I wasn't asking you out," Andrew said. "I was just giving you an example."

"Hercules?"

"A joke?"

"Knock it off before I put both of you in time-out. Look, Pea. Drew's right. Using nicknames for people you write about could be your *thing*. But *you* need to consider just being yourself."

She had no idea. "What I need is to go home to Noah."

"I'm sure the little matey is sound asleep by now," Andrew said.

"I know neither of you understands this, but soothing the woes of misbegotten middle-aged singles isn't my priority."

"Ouch. Your friend's brutal." Andrew cringed. "I should hire her for my litigation team."

"I thought you wanted to help me. I need your help moving forward, but we have to do things a little differently. We won't get you into any trouble," Jade said.

I wasn't sure she understood. I worked for the school district, I had an ex-husband. And parents. And a kid. "I do want to help you." I slowed my words. "I always want to help you if I can, but why do I have to use my real name?"

"Credibility," Andrew said. "And it's only a matter of time before someone figures it out anyway. It always happens."

"What is that supposed to mean?"

"Holden did some research about anonymous bloggers, and they rarely get more than six months under their belts before they admit who they are, or someone exposes them," Jade said. "Why not just do it yourself?"

I had no idea. "What is this really about?" I asked them both.

"It's about lots of things," Jade said. "Just keep an open mind. Please. We always wanted to find a way to work together. Now we have. Think of the possibilities."

Yes, they were endless. And awful.

"Even if I would agree to do this, and I'm not saying I will, I'm not going to suggest people get a divorce. That's not my place."

"Understood," Andrew said.

"Being a single parent sucks. People should avoid it if at all possible."

Andrew's hand reached halfway across the table, and then he pulled it back.

Andrew and I walked Jade to her car. I hugged her again, but she and Andrew just nodded and waved to each other. Then Andrew opened the passenger door of his SUV for me. "Thanks for taking me home."

"No problem. It would have been foolish to have Jade go out of her way just because you don't want to be in the car with me for ten or fifteen minutes."

I stepped up into the seat and noticed two car seats in the back.

Andrew walked around to the driver's side and climbed in.

"You have kids?"

"Yep."

"I didn't know."

"You didn't ask."

"I didn't think of it." That didn't come out as lighthearted as I'd intended. I didn't turn around but pictured the identical boosters. I glanced around the car for signs of errant Cheerios, or a lip gloss. A pink breast-cancer ribbon dangled from the rearview mirror.

"Meghan died almost three years ago."

He didn't need to say anything else.

"I'm sorry, Andrew. I didn't know."

"That's kind of a theme with you, isn't it?" He looked at me, and right into my eyes the way people say they do, but rarely *actually* do. Iris-to-iris contact. I gulped and turned my head to look out my window, discomfited yet calm.

I uttered my address without a sidebar or sarcasm. Andrew drove to Good Street in deliberate silence. After his SUV turned onto my block, I pointed to the right side of the street, then nodded when we double-parked near my house. I fumbled for more than my keys. An apology seemed immaterial, yet I *was* sorry. For what I'd said. For what Andrew and his children had lost. For my initial lack of tact. For my ongoing lack of perspective.

"Oh my God!"

"What?" Andrew jolted, and squeezed the steering wheel with both hands.

I pointed to the blue Honda parked ahead under the streetlight. "That's my ex-husband's car."

Chapter 21

Trouble

ANDREW PARKED AT THE far end of the street. I tempered my breathing to dull my nausea.

"You didn't know he was coming over?"

"I didn't know he was back from California."

"He moved to California?"

I turned my head and looked at Andrew. He looked at me, his expression solemn. I realized then that he knew nothing about me. Nothing true. "He was in Palo Alto. On business."

"Must've been hard on Noah. And you."

"You have no idea." As the words left my mouth, I tried to suck them back. "I'm sorry. That was a stupid thing to say."

Andrew raised and lowered one eyebrow, a trick I'd never mastered. "Don't worry about it. People say stupid things all the time."

"Gee, thanks."

"Not what I meant." He banged his head back on the headrest twice. "So, are we even?"

At ease, I smiled.

"How about if I walk you in? I have experience with ex-husbands."

"You have experience with ex-husbands?"

"I'm a divorce lawyer, remember?"

"Oh, right." Andrew Mann, attorney-at-law, was a divorce monger. Apparently, he was also a nice guy. Good thing, too, because at the moment I didn't want to face Bruce alone.

"You wouldn't mind walking in with me?"

"I wouldn't have offered if I minded."

I believed him. "Do you have a sitter or someone you need to call?"

"Nope, I've got everything under control. And don't worry, everything will be fine."

I believed him then, too.

I held my breath as tightly as I held my key.

"It's your house," Andrew whispered from behind me. His warm breath and encouraging words ruffled my hair and I shivered.

I unlocked my front door with one turn of the key, but pushed it open in slow motion. The door cooperated by not making a sound. I stepped out of the foyer and saw Bruce upright and asleep on the sofa. Noah's head, covered by my Phillies cap, rested on Bruce's lap.

"Do you want me to wake him up?" Andrew asked in a full, deep voice. I suspected it was his lawyer voice.

Bruce opened his eyes. He grinned at me as if he'd forgotten the babies, the marriage, and the divorce. He looked as if he were lounging on his bachelor-pad sofa, rising from a nap, still years from the cusp of an unimagined life. He dragged his hands down his face, and with the final swipe, drool lifted away from his mouth. His eyes circled as though he were laughing at himself, then he looked at Noah, back at me and Andrew, then at the drool on his sleeve, and frowned.

Embarrassed Bruce. I glanced back at Andrew and smiled. He'd removed his coat and draped it over the banister. I placed my hands on my hips and swiveled toward my ex, a calisthenics stance primed for a confrontation. But Bruce looked at Noah, then at me, and our unflappable parenting bond took hold. I wrapped my arms around myself and nodded. Bruce lifted Noah into his arms and stood. Noah rearranged himself without waking. He sank into Bruce as if he were a baby. Then, as if hopping on stones to cross a creek, Bruce took three, maybe four, steps at a time and disappeared upstairs. I offered no apologies for the laundry in the hall or the unmade beds.

"Way to take a stand there, Elizabeth," Andrew said.

"Noah was asleep, what was I supposed to do? And my name's Izzy."

"Uh-huh."

Bruce bopped down the steps and into the living room. I noticed his bright white socks and looked around the room to find his sneakers. He'd tucked them under the coffee table, heel to heel and toe to toe. How could someone have made such a mess of his life but always be certain to line up his shoes with precision?

I sat on the sofa, unsure of my next move, or word. Andrew flanked the dining and living rooms, taking up more man space than I'd have thought possible.

"Andrew Mann." He thrust his arm forward and walked toward Bruce.

They shook and nodded as if it were a business meeting and not an awkward quasi-personal moment.

"You look familiar." Bruce stepped back. He eyed Andrew straight on, then sideways. Bruce stood a head taller than Andrew, but from my perspective the disparity seemed negligible.

"What are you doing here?" I asked.

"What am I doing here? I told you I might be coming back. The question is, where the hell were you?" Bruce whisper-yelled and his nostrils flared as he glanced back at Andrew.

"Watch your mouth," Andrew said.

"Oh, I know who you are." Bruce pointed and wagged his finger. "You're that lawyer with the billboards. I can't believe *he's* your *Valentine*, Iz! Or is he your lawyer? Maybe he's both!"

"What he is, Bruce, is none of your business."

"Well, while you were out with *none-of-my-business,* your dear Mrs. Feldman vouched for me or that girl wouldn't have let me in to see my son."

"Had I known you were coming back, I'd have *let you* see Noah. You know that."

I knew Bruce well enough to know he was boiling inside. Bruce looked at Andrew and turned his head back and forth again as if he were counting. "What happened to that Mac guy?"

My body went cold and then hot and then cold again. I

couldn't move, didn't know what to say. Right there, in my parents'—*my*—living room, I was going to dissolve into the floor and become one with the Berber.

"Mac is out of the picture," Andrew said.

I fought to remain calm, my leg bounced harder and higher, and Bruce just stared at me and cocked his head, as if waiting for an apology.

"I was at a meeting, Bruce. Because I had to take a second job to make up for the money you stopped contributing to this household even though you're legally bound to do so."

"Don't start with that again, Izzy."

"You need to call before you come here. You can't just stop by. This is not your house, and I'm not at your beck and call. And neither is Noah."

"I figured you'd be here. I wanted to see Noah. Which I can do whenever I want."

I stood to defend myself, my space, my sanity. "No, you can't. Check our parenting agreement. You can see him every other weekend and Wednesday nights until Thursday before school. Would you like to see the custody agreement you signed? Maybe I'll underline the parts about child support. Do you have a highlighter handy? Or did you leave it in California?"

Bruce held up his hands, powerless to deflect the truth. "Look, I'm just saying that it's a bad idea to leave Noah with a stranger. I have no idea who that girl is. What if she's a lunatic?" Bruce sat on the sofa and jammed his feet into his sneakers.

"Are you kidding me? Was I never supposed to hire a sitter and leave the house? You've been away for six weeks."

"That was business."

"Tonight was business too. And Darby, that 'lunatic' babysitter you don't know, is a college graduate, and she works for Jade. She's not a stranger to me or to Noah." How does it feel not to know the all the people your child knows? That's what I wanted to ask him. Because I knew the answer. It felt as if you were standing outside the circle of your child's life, without the secret password or a ticket to get inside. And horrible as it may have been, I was glad Bruce was now feeling it too.

"So, what's this 'job' that keeps you out at night?" Bruce succumbed to using air quotes and glanced at Andrew.

"None of your business," I said.

And then I felt it. The burn in my throat, the pressure in my ears, the band of uncertainty around my heart. I hadn't cried in front of Bruce since the morning he woke up and said he was leaving. I wasn't going to start now. Plus, Andrew was here. I gulped and swallowed and turned away. I blew out enough air to fill a giant balloon, then turned back. My eyes filled but didn't betray me.

"I know you didn't want him, but you really shouldn't do things that make Noah feel that way."

"Knock it off!" Bruce spit the words through gritted teeth.

"What is he supposed to think, Bruce? You leave, you call—sometimes—and then you show up out of nowhere and want him for the weekend. What happens to Noah when you leave again?" And what happens to me?

Andrew turned and walked into the kitchen. I heard water running, a cabinet open and close. Then the refrigerator. The water stayed on.

"I don't want to hurt Noah. You know that. And I love that

kid. You know that. Stop throwing it in my face that *six years ago* I didn't think I wanted to be a dad. Just because I didn't want *us* doesn't mean I don't want Noah."

Don't scream. Don't cry. For God's sake, don't throw up.

Bruce's voice softened and he slipped his hands in his jeans pockets. "My lease is up and I'm putting my stuff in storage. I'm staying with my sister while I'm here. I'd like to pick up Noah in the morning and keep him through the weekend. I don't want to fight, Izzers. I just want to be the best dad I can be, and I'm trying. I know you don't believe this, but I don't want to fight with you either."

Tightness in my throat constricted my speech. If I opened my mouth, I'd squeak. Or bellow. Or rage.

I picked up Bruce's coat from the chair and handed it to him with resolve. "Fine. Come at noon." I slathered on the guilt. "He needs you to do more than swoop in and out like a superhero."

I shut the door behind Bruce, and Andrew emerged from the kitchen.

"I'm sorry," he said.

"You don't have anything to be sorry about."

"I'm sorry you're in this predicament. You know you can take him to court and get child support, right?"

"I know. But we're okay."

"That's not the point."

"I know."

"Well, just in case . . ." Andrew took a card out of his wallet, flipped it over, and scribbled on the back. He handed it to me and I slipped it into my pocket without making eye contact.

"Thanks for being here." And for running the water. And for not bolting. "And—thanks for not correcting Bruce when he assumed we were dating."

"No problem. What's a white lie between friends?"

The next day, I sat in Mrs. Feldman's living room, half-price Valentine's Day candy in one hand and Andrew's business card in the other.

"Oh, I love the Whitman's Sampler. My father used to buy them for us." Mrs. Feldman bit into a dark-chocolate raspberry cream. "Mmm! Now, what's in your other hand?"

The side with Andrew's chicken-scratched cell number was plain and matte. The other side was shiny and smooth, yet straightforward and classic.

ANDREW MANN

Attorney at Law

Mediation—Divorce—Adoption

I handed Mrs. Feldman the card. "Maybe you could talk to him about Elizabeth."

"No!" Mrs. Feldman pushed the card toward me and I sat on my hands. She placed the card on the coffee table. "I don't want anyone to know. I thought I made myself clear."

"He could help you. Look, it says 'adoption.' Andrew might be able to find Elizabeth. *Your* Elizabeth."

"*Your* Andrew? The one who helped with Bruce?"

My cheeks grew warm. "When I read the card last night, it hit me. He might be able find some answers. . . ."

"Please, no. I gave you the box and I told you because I knew you would keep my secret. I haven't told anyone what you've been doing. Please. Do the same for me."

"But maybe that's not the best thing. For either of us." I said the last part under my breath. This was about Mrs. Feldman, not me. "Maybe it's better to take the risk and tell the truth. What's the worst thing that could happen?" Mrs. Feldman crossed her arms and her fingers fluttered on her elbows. "Really? What's the worst thing?"

"We could find Elizabeth and she could hate me. She's seventy, for goodness' sake."

"We don't even know if we *can* find her, so let's not worry about that yet. One step at a time."

"The boys could stop talking to me if they find out."

We rolled our eyes simultaneously.

"I can just tell Andrew this is for 'a friend.' No names. He has never met you. He won't be able to figure anything out. And if he can't help, he won't know anything more. But if he can help . . ."

"Fine. Ask him. But after this, Elizabeth, it's your turn."

I already knew that.

Chapter 22

Hide-and-Seek

Mrs. Feldman reached into her purse and removed a dollar. "This seems silly." She smoothed the bill between her hands as if heating it up, before handing it to Andrew.

"No," he said. "Since you've paid me, I'm legally bound to keep everything said here today confidential. Would you like Ms. Lane to leave before we talk?"

"Hey!" I opened my mouth wide in shock and mild protest. I didn't expect to be offended, but I was. Many things were happening that I didn't expect. Such as Andrew calling me Ms. Lane.

"No, dear, Elizabeth can stay. She knows the whole story."

"Fine."

Andrew looked around the crowded dining-room table at his audience of figurines. Muted, pale, and refined—clowns holding balloons, ladies walking dogs, children playing games. I pulled out a chair and put Andrew's briefcase on it. He flipped the latch with his thumb, opened the case, and retrieved a yellow legal pad, seeming somewhat cliché.

Andrew didn't look at me, but leaned the pad on his arm. He faced Mrs. Feldman. "Start at the beginning."

Andrew nodded in time to her story. He scribbled on the paper, but from my spot at the end of the table, I couldn't make out what he was writing. For me, Mrs. Feldman had uttered no surprises. I continued placing Lladró into their appropriate boxes, comforted that the fragile nature of my wards was the only thing I'd been charged with protecting at the moment. I hoped she would choose her favorites to display in her apartment at Shady Forest, but maybe she wanted to leave it all behind, like her pirate box. I turned my back to offer the illusion of privacy.

"Elizabeth?" Andrew said.

I swiveled around without admonishing him for calling me Elizabeth. With him and Mrs. Feldman together, I'd be outvoted on my own name.

"Would you mind getting Mrs. Feldman's box? I'd like to catalog the contents, take some photos, just so I have a record of it."

"You can't open it," Mrs. Feldman said.

Andrew moved his case to the floor and pulled the chair closer to her. He sat and leaned forward, resting his arms on the table. Andrew appeared relaxed, yet in control. This posture had been well practiced.

"If you want my help, I need to know what's in there. It might help me find your daughter, Mrs. Feldman."

She winced. "You, too, with the *Mrs. Feldman*? It took Elizabeth almost forty years to call me Geraldine, and she only said it once, when she thought I was losing my mind. I'm not sure I have that much time to wait for you to do it, Mr. Mann."

Andrew laughed and blushed. "Okay, Geraldine. Then you have to call me Andrew."

Andrew snapped photos of the box from every angle. He measured it and jotted notes, numbers. He drew a diagram.

"I haven't opened that box since before my oldest was born," Mrs. Feldman said.

Andrew reached for her hand before I could. "You are the only one who knows what's in there. I can take it with me, open it, make note of the contents, and then give it back to Elizabeth if that would be easier for you."

"No." Mrs. Feldman shifted in the chair and tugged at her blouse. "It's fine. I'm making a lot of changes, moving from this house, you know." She motioned to the cardboard boxes and to me, still packing up Lladró. "Did Elizabeth tell you I was moving?"

"No, she didn't. But I assumed—"

"Of course you did. What would an old woman like me be doing living alone, right?"

"I didn't mean—"

"No, of course you didn't. The fact is, young man, we're not alone in this world unless we want to be. And living in this house, even with my tsuris, I've never been alone." Mrs. Feldman glanced at me and smiled. I knew she meant me, but not just me. Good Street, in its day, had a way of being a self-contained world filled with friends and reimagined family. "You know what tsuris is, dear?"

Andrew chuckled. *"Ikh farshteyn."*

"Ha! He understands a *pitseleh* Yiddish. A nice *Jewish* boy . . ." Mrs. Feldman looked right at me as she said it and her eyes opened wide. My cheeks grew so warm I thought I might be having my first hot flash. Great timing.

"Do you want me to go?" I did not look at Andrew, but pointed toward the door, hoping I could escape the heat along with all its implications.

"Heavens to Betsy, no! You're the only one besides Mr. Mann—I mean Andrew—who knows what happened. My shame should have died a long time ago. My hope should have gone with it, I know. But it didn't."

We moved to the kitchen table. After one silent turn of the key, Andrew lifted the lid. It folded all the way back as if gasping for its first breath. With slow, deliberate movements, Andrew laid out the contents of the box. First, four black-and-white photos. Then, a yellowed envelope with writing on the front.

Mrs. Feldman fiddled with her fingers in lieu of a napkin, turned back the edge of her cuff, then folded her hands. I wished Andrew would move just a little faster, without relaxing his care.

Two short, thick Shabbat candles. A wax-paper square that appeared to be folded, with something between the two pieces.

Mrs. Feldman pointed at the envelope. "Are you sure that's the box I gave you, Elizabeth?" She looked at me, nary a glint in her eye nor a smile on her lips.

I almost didn't know how to respond. The box sat on the table. The box that had been locked for decades and had only recently found a home in my bread/hat/note drawer.

"Of course it is."

"Well, I don't remember putting any envelope in there, I'll

tell you that. The rest of it, yes. But the envelope? No. Although it was a long time ago." She fanned out the photos but did not lift them from their places.

"What's in the wax paper?" I asked. Mrs. Feldman wouldn't answer if she didn't want me to know.

"A piece of my hair."

"That's very smart," Andrew said. "We can use it for DNA testing. If there's ever a reason, of course."

"I just did it so my daughter would have a piece of me. There was none of that DNA testing back then. I didn't even know there was something called DNA."

"Well, it was good thinking."

"What about the envelope?" I prodded Andrew with a jut of my chin. He lifted the envelope and showed it to Mrs. Feldman. "It says *Geri* on the front."

"Sol is the only one who called me Geri." Mrs. Feldman wrung her hands. "Open it." Her words squeaked through the breath of a whisper.

I laid my hand on her back, using pressure to steady her body. I leaned closer to steady her heart, and the imagined shield drifted away.

June 10, 1954

Dearest Geri,

Your cousin Myrna told me everything.

I think she wanted to drive me away, to punish you somehow. (Myrna was never very kind-hearted, you told me that.) But of course nothing could take me away from you. I'm glad I know about your baby girl. I'm glad I know where you go when you stare out the window. I'm glad I know why you are a little bit sad every holiday and every year on March 8th. But I'm sorry you felt you couldn't tell me, that you didn't have enough faith in me, and in us. Just say the word and I will help you find your daughter. We will go to Staten Island and to that hospital and demand answers. You deserve to know that she is safe and loved. She deserves to know you are her real mother. I will take you away from this house and this street and we will start a new life somewhere else where you don't have to keep any secrets from anyone. Just say the word.

Until then, I shall not mention it again, ever. Your secret is safe with me, as is your heart.

Your loving husband,

Sol

"Everything could have been different. Why didn't he just tell me?" Mrs. Feldman touched her cheeks with both hands and shook her head. She furrowed her brows, as if translating words from a foreign language. "I didn't have to carry this alone all these years. Oh, Sol, why didn't you tell me?"

Andrew slipped the letter into the envelope and slid it across the table. Then he placed each item back into the box, closed the lid, but didn't lock it.

My throat ached with the weight of a sheltered sob. From behind, I squeezed Mrs. Feldman's shoulders in a gentle hug and kissed her cheek. She grasped my hands.

Andrew spoke into the air, as if to no one. "Secrets and lies change lives. And rarely in a good way."

His words burst like soap bubbles and stung my eyes.

Chapter 23

Duck, Duck, Goose

THIS WAS IT. THE day of reckoning. I'd had time to consider Jade's offer and to think about what it could mean moving forward. And it did seem like moving forward, which is what I wanted and needed. The money would be crucial if Bruce couldn't get a job. And if he did? With Bruce's child support I could save a little every month. I brightened at the thought of a nest egg, a vacation fund, of feeling secure. I would accept Jade's job as the new Dear Abby. But first, I had to come clean.

I scanned the dining room for Jade and Rachel. There they were, sitting and sipping, engrossed in conversation. Next, I scanned for emotional emergency exits. This was going to be tough. As I made my way over to the table, I saw coordinated couples at tables for two, clusters of friends tucked into corner booths, long tables accommodating multigenerational families. I heard chatter absorbed by well-planned acoustics, and servers who wove seamlessly among the guests.

What would people see at our table? Jade, the stunning

workaholic growing a business but not a personal life? Rachel, the soccer mom who had flirted with disaster? Me, liar, liar, pants on fire?

I plopped myself down and poured myself a glass of wine. Then I plucked an olive from Jade's plate and popped it into my mouth.

Jade lifted her wineglass to the center of the table. "Here's to—opportunities!"

"Yes, to opportunities." Rachel clinked her wineglass with Jade's.

I tipped my glass forward and clinked it with Rachel's, as we had throughout our childhoods. Milk, soda, juice, water. Glass, plastic, paper, aluminum. It didn't matter. I picked up the menu.

"Everything looks good. We're sharing plates, right?"

"Don't rush." Jade pushed down my menu. "You don't have a curfew."

"Right." Noah was with Bruce.

"This is the good part," Rachel said. "You get time off."

"I know."

"Well, I'll be taking less time off in the future," Jade said. "I have news."

"So do I," I said. "But you go first."

"I'm not supposed to tell anyone this yet because all the papers aren't signed, but . . ." Jade leaned forward almost into the olives. "I'm selling Pop Philly."

"What?"

"I'm tired of worrying about a new influx of cash. I didn't want to sell ads, I wanted to create great content. *The Philadel-*

phia Press made me an offer I couldn't refuse." Her imitation of Marlon Brando set us onto a detour of girlish giggles.

I exhaled to gain composure. "How did this happen?"

"They'd been coming to me for the past year and I kept saying no. I didn't want to sell out."

"What changed?"

"You did."

"I made you want to sell Pop Philly?"

"In the last few months our numbers have skyrocketed. The *Press* upped their offer. I'd have been a fool to say no. Drew vetted the whole thing for me."

"What does this mean?" I shivered as a cold rush flowed through me.

"I'm going to stay on as editor in chief and do what I wanted to do all along. Don't worry, your job still stands. *You* made this possible!"

Mrs. Feldman would say, *It's an ill wind that blows no good.* Or maybe she would just say, *Oy vey.*

"You, my dear friend, are going to be Dear Izzy in a new advice column in all these new cities." Jade opened her arms wide as if revealing the prize behind door number three. "It's a great opportunity!"

"If the *Press* owns Pop Philly, who would I be working for?"

"Me! As editor in chief I'll be in charge of building the hyper-local markets with the *Press*'s parent company. And I won't have to worry about the advertising or the technical side of things." At this Jade pretended to wipe sweat from her brow. "They have papers and Web sites in ten major markets—all the places your column will be featured, on their sites and advertised in their print editions."

"What about the rest of the team? What's going to happen to Holden? And Darby?"

"Holden found a new job. When the *Press* first started sniffing around for real, I pulled him aside and told him about it. He's as solid as they come. And I'm glad I did, because the *Press* has a whole tech staff and they weren't hiring anyone new. He's a great kid, really talented, and I wanted to be up-front with him. He'll be with me through the transition and then he's moving to San Francisco. He landed a job with Google."

"Is Darby going with him?"

Jade read my thought bubble. "They're not a couple. Holden's like a mentor to her, a big brother."

"Oh! They seem like a couple. They're together all the time."

"She relies on him, looks up to him. Darby worked her way through community college, works at Starbucks full-time, and for Pop Philly part-time. I know she really wanted to be the dating blogger, and I saw her practically salivate over the idea of an advice column, but I saved that for you. I'll find something else for her to do if she's still interested. After everything's out in the open."

There was my sign, handed to me on a silver platter and sprinkled with olives. I sipped my wine and changed the subject instead. "But if you're not monitoring the business end of things with Pop Philly anymore, what? What happens to Andrew? Will he still be advertising on the site? Will he still be working with us? I mean, you?"

"Okay, missy. Since when do you care so much about *Andrew*?" Jade said.

"I thought you said he was a jerk?" Rachel said. "Obviously not if he's helping Jade."

And Mrs. Feldman. And me.

"He's a good guy," Jade and I said together. I covered my mouth with my hand, and Jade's lips turned up into a smile.

"Well, well," she said.

"People aren't always who you think they are, are they?" Rachel made it sound like a question, but I knew it was a statement.

"Talk her into it while I'm gone." Jade left the table for the ladies' room.

"You should've told Jade your news first," Rachel said.

"You can see how excited she is. This is everything she ever wanted. She deserves her own happily ever after."

"So you're willing to keep this up?"

"For now."

If it helped Jade, then, yes. I'd put my lies behind me without confessing.

"What are you going to do?" I asked.

"About what?"

"About Jeremy!"

"It was harder than I thought, but I deleted my Facebook account. Then I blocked his number from my phone. I feel like I'm going through withdrawal. I check my phone every two minutes even though I know he can't text me."

"You did the right thing."

"When I told Seth we need to go to counseling, he said, 'I know.' "

"You told him about Jeremy?"

"Not yet. But I will when the time is right."

I squeezed Rachel's hand and tried to absorb some of her bravery.

Jade slid back into her seat. "Well? Are you in?"

I was, but not the way she thought. "Can I have a few days to think about it?"

"Sure. But there *is* another very important topic we need to discuss right now."

"What might that be?"

"Your fortieth birthday."

— Chapter 24 —

Charades

BRUCE TIPPED HIS COWBOY hat. He had a DEPUTY badge clipped to his coat; Noah's badge said SHERIFF. Noah looked up at his dad. Bruce glanced down, smiled, and pushed Noah's matching hat down over his eyes. Noah threw back his head and galloped into the living room, exuberant as only a five-year-old can be.

In two days, Noah's allegiance had shifted from pirates to cowboys. Or was that mom to dad? Little boys yearned to be like their father, and at five they wanted *to be* their father. Even my brothers, who had no interest in inheriting Lane Hardware, mimicked our dad in style and in stance throughout their lives. I'd seen many black-and-white photos of Dad with little Eddie and little Ethan in their masculine store aprons and tool belts. By the time I was old enough to sit at the store and observe, Dad all but pounded his chest when the boys traipsed the aisles straightening cans of spray paint or explained to puzzled customers the difference between lag and hex bolts. Pound, pound, pound. Even now, if my dad and brothers sat in the same room for more than twenty minutes, they'd find a 1980s episode of *This Old House* to watch in bonded silence, right leg crossed on left, hands behind their heads.

Noah deserved a dad whose life hinged on being his son's father. I hung up Noah's coat and glanced back at Bruce. I hadn't noticed the tinge on his cheeks Friday night, but Bruce's face glowed with more of a bottled tan than a California one. Faint lines accented his eyes, exacerbated by his squinting as if he needed glasses. Bruce removed his coat, then his hat, but held them. I traced his shoulders with my thoughts, but inside maintained a steady heartbeat. Just two months ago I'd have wrestled away thoughts of the fabric and fit and what lurked beneath. I'd have blushed. Today I didn't care, just wanted Bruce to leave so I could be with Noah.

The opposite of love was not hate. The opposite of love was not sarcastic retorts. The opposite of love was not spiteful thoughts. The opposite of love—this love—was indifference.

I rubbed the back of my dry neck. I didn't care what Bruce had, where he went, what he did, or whom he did it with—unless it affected Noah. There were many overlaps, but now, clear distinction. The lines in my life were no longer ambiguous.

"Are you listening to me?" Bruce snapped.

"Yes. Sorry," I lied. Twice.

"I said *I'm staying.*" Bruce placed a plastic supermarket bag on the floor. Noah's clothes peeked out the top. "It's all clean."

His statements shuffled and I wasn't sure which to address first. "Clean clothes?"

"Yes."

"So, your sister did the laundry."

"Does matter who did the laundry? I brought back clean clothes."

"Thanks." I meant it. "What did you mean, you're staying?" I leaned back against the closed closet, disinviting Bruce deeper into my house. Or my life.

"I'm staying here. At my sister's."

"I didn't forget where you were, Bruce."

"I mean I'm staying longer. Until I find a new place of my own."

Wednesday nights, every other weekend, child-support checks. Images of Noah and Bruce getting into his car, driving away, flashed in front of me. My insides twisted, but just for a second, as the euphoric sensation of Sunday-night homecoming hugs resurfaced. "So, you found a job?"

"I did. It's not exactly what I wanted, but . . ." Bruce looked into the living room at Noah.

Bruce wanted Noah more than he wanted the perfect job.

I choked back words of pride, but felt a swell in my chest instead of a snarky comeback.

"What about Amber?" I wasn't asking as Bruce's ex-wife. I was asking as Noah's mom. The question had no undercurrent. When Bruce just stared at me without snarling, I knew he felt that, too. "I mean, if you're not seeing her anymore, you should probably tell Noah. He liked her."

Bruce looked at me, his brow furrowed slightly, as if he didn't realize he was thinking.

"We'll figure that out."

I didn't know who he meant by *we,* and I didn't ask.

"I wanted to tell you, I'm not going to be traveling anymore.

This is an office job," he said. "So now I want Noah fifty percent of the time."

"What?"

"Fifty percent. Either half of each week or every other week. We can see which works better."

Neither. "No."

"What do you mean, no?"

"I'm the residential parent, Bruce." I rubbed my fingers into my palms to stop my hands from shaking.

"I checked with my lawyer. You can still be the residential parent, Noah won't change schools, but we already share custody. I have the legal right to have Noah for as much time as you do."

"Unless you change your mind and go away for six weeks, right?"

"How do I know you're not out every night and leaving Noah with a babysitter? And Friday night you came home with that guy. Did he sleep here? What if Noah would have walked downstairs after I'd left? What kind of an example is *that* for Noah?"

My anger swelled. "There is no comparison to a weeknight meeting and six weeks in California. And Andrew only came into the house because I saw your car."

"You needed backup? Really? I'm not a monster, Izzers. I'm his dad."

"You're not taking him away from me."

"And you can't keep him from me."

"What happens when the West Coast calls again? Or you get fired again?"

Bruce's neck reddened. "I'm not going anywhere, Iz."

"Famous last words." When I was pregnant each time, I'd sworn I'd be an ever-present parent. Could I be present when Noah and I were apart as much as we were together? I would have to be. I didn't want Noah to Ping-Pong between us, but he already was. "This is not what we agreed on. You were just fine with your Wednesday night and every other weekend. And so was Noah. He was fine until you left again."

"I missed him, Iz. I want to be a full-time dad, not a Disney dad." Someone had been reading parenting books. "Let's not end up in court. Fathers have rights."

"Fathers have rights *and obligations*!"

"California was a mistake. Haven't you ever done something you wish you could take back?"

Jerk.

"This isn't about how you feel about me, it's about Noah."

Of course it was about Noah. But it was also about me. What would I do if I weren't a full-time mommy? Who would fill the hours between dinner and bedtime? Who would I give Eskimo kisses every morning? Who would I read to and snuggle with and kiss on the top of the head? I didn't know who I was without Noah. I wasn't sure I wanted to know.

"Noah needs to be with me as much as he needs to be with you," Bruce said.

Had Bruce just realized this? Where was this reasoning when he broke up our family? Skipped Wednesday-night dinners? Took off with Amber? I wanted to protect Noah from the heartbreak and disappointment. That was my job.

But as much as I hated to admit it, I believed Bruce. For better or worse, he was back for good.

I'd forgotten the rush of maternal adrenaline that came with seeing Noah after a night apart. I'd feel that more often when Noah was with Bruce half the time. Though it was nearing bedtime, and tomorrow was another school day for us both, I ached to stretch the next hour into two. I wouldn't rush through stories, skip pages, or suggest he looked oh so tired. I would savor each word, syllable, and finger-licked turn of the page. Noah stacked books on his nightstand with care, as if building a house of cards.

I sat on Noah's bed and shimmied back against the pillow and headboard. He sat next to me. "You might be more comfortable without the cowboy hat." Noah shook his head and held the hat on. "The hat is awesome, but you know what I think would be more awesome?"

"What?"

"If tonight we weren't cowboys or pirates."

"Or Spider-Man?"

"That's right."

"Who do you want to be?" Noah's eyes stretched wide and round.

That was a very good question. "I just want to be Noah and Mommy."

Noah nodded, removed the hat, and nuzzled against my side and into the crook of my arm with a book in his hands. He announced the title and author as if hosting *Masterpiece*

Theatre, then began reading—reciting—a story he knew by heart.

I wasn't holding the book, nor was I reading it. He was reading to me. I participated with my attentive silence. Then my mind drifted to the day Noah had held his bottle for the first time. What was my job now? I thought it then and today. Noah pointed to words and pronounced each one he knew. His *r*'s sounded more and more like *r*'s than they ever had before. Each milestone of independence liberated and debilitated me. I kissed his forehead twice and his face turned up toward mine.

After the divorce, the childhood I imagined and then sowed for Noah had been remnants of my own. That's all I could imagine. I had claimed the move to Good Street was for Noah, so that he'd have the comforting childhood I'd had with close-knit neighbors, games of half-ball, and summer nights sitting on the steps until way past dark waiting for our parents to call it a night and call us inside. I wanted Noah to collect those memories like the seashells we gathered down the shore and used for craft projects that were stacked on shelves and safeguarded in dusty boxes. But Noah wasn't going to grow up with two parents in the same house, or with two older brothers. He was going to have *two* homes, no siblings. Kids didn't knock on each other's door anymore. Parents didn't sit out on the steps. Teenagers didn't throw Converses over the telephone wires anymore. No one knew telephones once needed wires.

Noah's childhood needed to be Noah's—filled with experiences unencumbered by my rewound memories or idyllic expectations. His future was unwritten and propitious.

And if I allowed it, so was mine.

Chapter 25

Truth or Dare

THE RED-CARPETED STAIRS AND the canopied portico of the Pinnacle Hotel had always reminded me of an old-fashioned carousel, but with dapper doormen instead of carnival barkers, revolving doors instead of painted ponies. Just like during my childhood adventures at Playland, I fidgeted as I waited my turn to go in. It was just like Jade to choose my favorite place in Center City to celebrate my birthday.

I inhaled the warming winter air before ascending the stairs, looking ahead instead of at my feet. The three-inch heels were bearable—so far. I squinted and saw Holden on the other side of the glass. The attendant held open a side door. I kept pace as I floated inside, onto an opulent, colorful fleur-de-lis carpet.

Fancy, schmancy, as Mrs. Feldman would say.

Holden met me as I stepped inside. "I tried to call you today. We need to talk."

With my hands in the air, I traced the outline of my silhouette. "*This* takes time. Plus, I knew I'd see you tonight." I smiled at my own wit and charm. "I'm glad you're here."

Holden didn't smile, but held out his arm, an invitation to give him my coat. So I did. "You look very nice." He said it as if I were a four-year-old who had dressed in a tutu for the eighth day in a row.

Looping my arm with his, Holden steered me toward an alcove filled with a floral arrangement the size of my kitchen table. I touched a magenta petal. It was silky and real. The flowers ranged from deep pinks to shadowy oranges, the foliage full and opaque. It was tropical and playful, yet somehow majestic. I quavered, feeling a bit underdressed and bleak by comparison.

"We need to talk before you go in there," Holden said.

"Okay, but I need to talk to Jade. Do you know where she is?"

"There you are!" Holden and I turned toward the lobby.

Jade walked like a model, placing her heel directly in front of the other foot's toes. But Jade didn't stride, she strolled. Her natural cadence mesmerized me. I'd worn black. Jade had worn winter white. Black and white. Good and evil. Darby scampered about a half step behind my best friend, trying to catch up.

Darby at my birthday dinner? Really, Jade? She sometimes took this mentor thing too far.

"I'm on time," I said, tapping my watchless wrist.

"Yes, you are. And you look stunning!" Jade hugged me the way she did on special occasions; affection resided in her actions, and in her eyes. "Well, come on, birthday girl, let's go in."

"No 'birthday girl' until tomorrow, thank you very much. I'm milking my thirties until the last possible second."

Andrew appeared behind Darby.

Now, *he* was a welcome addition to the guest list.

I'd grown accustomed to seeing Andrew in khakis or jeans and oxford-cloth shirts, the occasional polo. Tonight he was wearing a subtle plaid sport coat and tie, with a white shirt that had either been starched or was new. I placed my hands low on my hips, then behind my back. Then in front me. I'd forgotten how good some men looked dressed up. And apparently I'd also forgotten what to do with my hands.

"I told Jade you weren't going to like this change in tonight's plans." Andrew raised and lowered his eyebrows at Jade in a silent reprimand. On my behalf or on his own? I wasn't sure.

"What change?"

"You haven't told her?"

His ardent demeanor flustered me and I shifted my eyes back to Jade, my heart pounding with curiosity. Yes, curiosity. That was it. I was ready to tell Jade about Mac and accept the *Dear Izzy* job. I just needed a few minutes alone with her before dinner.

"What haven't you told me? I thought we were here to celebrate my birthday."

"We are," Jade said. "Sort of."

I placed a cold, wet towel on the back of my neck. Thank goodness for the accoutrements of upscale ladies' rooms.

"I promise," Jade said. "It'll be great. It's just a little party—well, not little."

"How many people are in there?"

"I don't know."

"About sixty," Darby said.

"Sixty? I thought there would be, like, I don't know . . . ten? Who on earth did you invite?"

"Ethan."

"Who else? Jade—tell me."

"My new bosses from the *Press*. And readers. And your friends from work. I'm going to make a big announcement about the Web site and about you! Won't that be a great way to turn forty—by letting the cat out of the bag?"

"You can't do that!"

"What do you mean I can't? I did. My bosses are thrilled. I told them everything."

Not everything. I grabbed Jade's forearm and she patted my hand.

"It'll be fine. Take a minute to regroup. I'm going to get back in there, make sure the hors d'oeuvres are being passed and the drinks are flowing."

My confession would have to wait until after dinner. I'd go in there, keep to myself, mingle as little as possible, and nod when Jade mentioned my name. I could muster a Miss America wave to be social. For Jade I could do that. For Jade I had to do that.

Darby had tucked herself into the corner of the ladies' room, out of the way, but now she'd been charged with my care and delivery. The room spun and I rearranged my reality.

"Just be yourself." Darby walked over and looked at me in the mirror. "You're forty. How hard could that be?"

The bitch had no idea.

Darby checked her watch and I noticed her tattoo, on the

inside of her forearm: CARPE DIEM. Yes. I would. I would seize the day. Just a little later than planned.

"It's time," Darby said.

"I'll be ready in a minute."

"I mean it's time to come clean."

"What are you talking about?" My throat was dry. I needed some water. No, I needed wine.

"I know about Mac."

"Everybody knows about Mac."

"No, I *know* about Mac. He was always too good to be true."

Too good to be true, indeed.

Darby held out her arm: CARPE DIEM. With a capital C and D. *CD.*

"You were CD!"

"I was."

"But you stopped."

"Because I had bigger plans."

"The new advice column. You want that job for yourself."

"I deserve that job. I've earned it. That's what makes us different."

And about a million other things. Starting with the nose ring.

"It's your word against mine when it comes to Mac, Darby. Who do you think Jade will believe?"

"I took photos of the notes I found in your 'bread drawer.'"

"You went into the drawer in my kitchen?" Right. Noah was wearing my Phillies cap when I came home and found him with Bruce. Darby had scooped the hat out of the drawer along with intel.

She rolled her eyes, reminded me she was more of an adolescent than an adult. "It's a bread drawer. I didn't expect to find evidence. I expected to find *bread*."

She couldn't have gone looking for ice cream?

I made eye contact with Darby, maybe for the first time ever. "You're too late. I'm telling Jade about Mac after dinner."

"No, *you're* too late. I'm telling everyone in that room how you lied—and I don't know—maybe telling how Jade was in on it to fool the readers and land this new big deal with the *Press*—*unless* you tell her you're not taking the job, *and* that you think I should be the new advice columnist. I don't care what reason you give her, or what you tell her or don't tell her after that."

"I can't make her hire you. And—that's extortion!"

"That's real life."

Darby walked out in a cloud of arrogance, then the handicapped-accessible stall door opened. Out walked Mrs. Feldman.

Her easy smile and familiar gait calmed me, and I filled with relief as if someone had turned on a spigot. She walked toward the sinks but stopped in front of me. She pointed her finger close to my nose, which tingled with a mix of fear and anticipation.

"Don't worry, Elizabeth. We'll fix *her* wagon."

I counted to twenty, then opened the door. The space sparkled and sizzled under the glow of a dimmed chandelier. People were milling, sitting, talking, laughing, eating, drinking. I stood still, my feet heavy with the weight of decision. Determined, I walked through the room, but no one acknowledged me. Of course not. I wasn't wearing a Phillies cap. I didn't see Jade. I didn't see Holden or Andrew. Was I in the right place? I scanned faces looking for someone familiar, and then, the Lane family aura permeated the air and grabbed me. Toward the back of the room I saw Ethan. Then I saw Eddie. I noticed the back of a woman next to Eddie. Trish. Then I spotted Rachel and Seth, her arm linked through his and holding tight. Jade waved to me from her perch at a high top. Next to her were my nephew, Matthew, and my niece Brooke. Donna and Helen and—Dr. Howard from Liberty? And he was wearing a black suit with a red tie. He looked almost trendy. They stood nearby with champagne flutes and smiles. I swiveled, feeling as if *now* anywhere I looked, I'd see someone else I hadn't expected. I saw Andrew, whom I *had* expected, with his hand in his pants pocket, other hand moving in time to words I couldn't hear, standing with Mrs. Feldman.

Still, I felt like a bride at a shotgun wedding. Not one thing was as it should have been. I was all dressed up, ready to get on with it. There was nowhere to hide. I grabbed a glass of red wine from a passing tray and walked toward Mrs. Feldman. Andrew had just walked away.

"I was just telling Andrew how lovely the party is and how happy I am to be here."

"Are you sure that's all you told him?"

"The rest is up to you. And no matter what happens next, this is the right thing to do right now."

Andrew returned holding a cocktail, but not the foo-foo umbrella kind.

"I'm going to leave you two." Mrs. Feldman held my hand until our arms were outstretched and we were too far apart.

I was now alone with Andrew in a room filled with people. "Thanks for helping her look for her daughter."

"No problem."

Is that all he could say? I was trying to make conversation. Andrew was not cooperating with my weak attempts to flirt or to distract myself from what I was about to do.

I finished my wine in one gulp. I should have told him right then. There was no Mac. I loved kids. I wanted to date a man who was a father. But all I could think was, why did I wear these stupid heels? I'd always dated tall men. I married a tall man, so that was no real measure for success. Did it matter if I was taller than Andrew? No, we weren't dating. But if we were? We weren't. At the moment I wasn't even talking to Andrew. I kicked off my pumps toward the wall. "I don't know why women wear these things."

Andrew chortled and shook his head. I could have blamed it on the wine, but why bother? It was just the beginning. There was more emotional disrobing to come.

I couldn't get Jade alone before she walked to the front of the room, evoking a *Norma Rae* vibe. She spoke fervently about the merger of Pop Philly with *The Philadelphia Press,* and the crowd cheered. She lauded the new Web sites and introduced local editors from South Jersey, DC, Columbus, Pittsburgh, and Boston. This was her baby, and I'd been careless with it.

My legs shook under my table. Rachel sat to my right, her

hand patting my back. Her other hand held Seth's. With Ethan on my left, we scrolled through the newest Maya photos, as well as plans for her birthday party. I was in charge of purple balloons, and it lifted me like helium, just for that moment. Eddie, Trish, Matthew, and Brooke sat with Mrs. Feldman and my Liberty High contingent. Surely I wasn't being fired if my boss was drinking champagne in my honor.

I laid my head on Ethan's shoulder. I could have told him my plan. But then he'd have stopped me.

"And now," Jade said, "I'd like to talk about one of our newer and more popular features on Pop Philly, our *Philly over Forty* blog."

Everyone clapped. Of course they did. I saw Darby on the other side of the room staring at Jade. Darby wouldn't do anything while Jade was talking, would she?

"While this started as a way to engage a new demographic for Pop Philly, it has really taken on a life of its own, so much so that we're introducing an advice column for the rollout of our newly designed site and all our affiliates."

Jade looked at me and nodded.

"If you're here, you probably know that the face of *Philly over Forty* wasn't a face, it was a Phillies cap." A Phillies cheer erupted that had nothing to do with me. The crowd quieted. "We agreed to keep the identity of the blogger a secret for the past two months because this person had a lot going on, but more than that, she has insight and humor and a dedication to helping others."

Dig the knife in deeper, Jade, please. I can't feel it.

"And this same person is going to be our new advice columnist. So, please welcome Izzy Lane. And give her a big round of applause. Tomorrow is Izzy's fortieth birthday, so it's a really special night for her."

I stood at my seat and looked around the table, knowing Darby was watching me, waiting. I looked at her and flashed a toothy, fake smile.

I walked toward Jade and she started clapping and sat in her seat. Everyone clapped and some people high-fived me. I felt as if I were on *The Price Is Right,* when, really, everything was wrong.

When I got to the front of the room, I looked at Jade and mouthed, *I'm sorry.* Then I looked out into the crowd.

"It's true. My name is Izzy Lane. Actually, Elizabeth Lane." I glanced at Andrew. "And what's also true is—tomorrow I turn forty." Now I didn't look at anyone, just straight ahead into the room at large.

My heart pounded so loud in my chest I feared I was screaming my words above the noise. I couldn't modulate my voice, or my thinking. "I loved writing *Philly over Forty,* sharing my stories with other single women, and some men, and most of all connecting with the readers. All of you, you're the ones who made me okay with being here now. And I don't mean at the Pinnacle drinking champagne. I mean here, where I am in my life. Single. Forty. You all know *a lot* about me. That's definitely true, please don't doubt that. But there is something you don't know. . . ."

I looked across the room at Mrs. Feldman. She gave me a

thumbs-up, as if I were about to take off in a single-engine plane and fly across the Atlantic. Except this was scarier.

And then I thought of Noah. He deserved a mother who *liked* what she saw when she looked in the mirror; who didn't make-believe, except as part of a game; who didn't build worlds, except out of LEGOs.

"What you don't know about me is that I lied." I looked at Darby, whose eyes were wide as a Kewpie doll's, and then looked back into imagined nothingness in front of me. "And I lied about more than my name. But I did that on my own. Jade had nothing to do with this. Nothing. She didn't know until now, like all of you. She just wanted to help me. And she did. But what I did was wrong. I just didn't realize how wrong until it was too late."

The room was quiet. I looked down at my bare feet and wiggled my toes. I'd never slipped back on my shoes. I needed a pedicure. Would anyone notice? Sentences rattled in my brain, and their echoes dizzied me. I sweated. I fanned the back of my neck. I unzipped my dress along its side to let in the air, exposing my skin to anyone who dared watch. My dress touched the top of my knees but I shimmied it up higher, and my legs burned to the touch. But when I watched myself from above, I was staring straight ahead, zipped up and coiffed. Then, back on the ground, looking down at my feet again, I heard words outside myself. Full sentences leaving my mouth without my consent, as if Balloons the Clown were pulling a string of primary-colored scarves out of his sleeve. One after another after another. I was the one talking, but I only heard bits and pieces of my voice. I covered my ears with my hands at my sides and kept talking. . . .

The Good Neighbor

Blog
Soccer
Amber
Bruce
Envy
Sadness
Mac
Escape
Snowball
Confession
Embarrassment
Lasagna
California
Money
Pop Philly
Geraldine
Readers
Comments
Donna
Ethan
Excitement
Relationships
Confusion
Notes
Stories
Snowball
Popularity
Guilt
Shame

Rachel

Concession

Remorse

Column

Chances

Jade

Opportunity

Noah

Spider-Man

Dear Izzy, Jade, Darby

And then, with nothing left to lose, I looked up.

"The truth is . . ." No one snickered. "I hated everything about my life."

Impeccable timing for *that* revelation.

"Even with a job I loved and a great kid and amazing friends and a family who loves me. And when you feel that way, crazy things happen. I was embarrassed that my ex had a girlfriend and I was alone." Jade turned away. I willed her to look at me, into the same eyes she'd looked into when she held my hand all night after my miscarriage. I was that person now. Off course. Shattered. Straddling realities. "Then I was embarrassed I lied about it. Embarrassed I kept lying. I lied to protect an ego I didn't even have. Really, I didn't need protection from anyone but myself. I put Jade and Pop Philly in jeopardy because I was embarrassed." I transferred my gaze to the table of *Press* executives. "I wish I had had the guts to not just come clean, but to never do this in the first place. I wish I thought it was okay to just be upset that my ex had a girlfriend and that it made me feel like crap. I didn't even want to get divorced." I just said *crap* in the middle of the Pinnacle Hotel and admitted that my ex had summarily dumped me. I looked back at my feet, still as unsightly as the rest of me. "If you learn anything from this, it is that trying to hide who you are or even what you've done? Never a good idea. Secrets and lies don't protect you, they strip you bare. And one more thing. I don't deserve to write for Pop Philly anymore, but neither does Darby Bartlett." I told them why.

Carpe diem, indeed.

Everyone was silent and still for what seemed like forever. I felt the ripples of the carpet beneath my feet. Without looking I felt Jade leave the table in front of me. Without looking I also knew the footsteps going after her were Andrew's.

— *Chapter 26* —

Mystery Date

Now I was in the lobby without my shoes or my handbag. I also didn't have my phone, my keys, or my pride. I trembled as I walked into the Pinnacle's lobby bar. I sat on a leather club chair at a table in the corner and slid my hands under my thighs to stop their shaking. The bartender nodded but didn't speak, his people-reading skills above reproach. My thoughts quieted even though guests filled most of the other tables. I blew out a stream of shame, further deflating my ego and consciousness. No windows were around me, just a wall lined with books and an archway leading back to the lobby. It could have been any day, anytime, anyplace, so I pretended for a moment that I'd intentionally stopped for a drink without my shoes, as if a thirsty, tired flower child. Then, the bartender placed a cosmopolitan in front of me in an etched martini glass with a twisted stem. It was pretty and pink and very much something to be consumed with shoes on. I crossed my ankles and drew back my legs.

"It's your birthday, right?"

I nodded.

"Compliments of the house, then, ma'am."

Ma'am? If he was trying to make me feel better, *that* wasn't helping. But it wasn't his fault I was almost forty, and it wasn't his fault I was here in his bar, alone and barefoot, bare everywhere. "Thank you." I nodded and sipped my pretty pity drink as he walked away.

Honesty was freeing, no matter its vessel, yet it also carried with it the weight of disappointment and expectation—mine and others'. I looked at the glass's round indentation on the napkin and I pushed my finger along the circle, tearing it. So much for fancy napkin folding. I crumbled the pieces and left them on the table, knowing that every trace of my minutes at that table would be erased as soon as I'd left. Some things could be undone and others couldn't.

I noticed Darby on the other side of the room, at a table but facing the wall. I wished I'd never met her. Or that Noah hadn't liked her enough for me to let her babysit. But everything that led to tonight was my fault, not hers.

I stood behind Darby but she didn't turn around. "Why didn't you tell Jade when you found out about Mac?"

"Because Holden said he'd tell her I was the one writing those comments, and she'd fire me. Which she just did."

One thousand points for Holden.

A zillion for Jade.

The lobby splayed in front of me like a Broadway stage filled with dancers. I searched for Jade amid the bodies and faces of the people walking, sitting, and standing. I needed to know if I'd lost my best friend. But to do that, I'd have to find her.

I sat on the bottom step of a wide, carpeted, curving staircase leading to the mezzanine. As I scanned the hotel guests and a crowd of bridesmaids in navy taffeta, I knew what else I had to do. I had to pay back the money Jade had given me. As soon as Bruce was working again and helping take care of Noah, I'd clip coupons, eliminate cable, and increase the deductible on my car insurance. I should have taken those steps two months ago, but I didn't want to give up anything else when I felt as if I'd lost so much.

I had no idea how much more there was to lose.

Now, if Noah had what he needed, nothing else mattered. I'd use the time Noah was with Bruce to bring in extra money. I had no idea what I'd do, but it didn't matter. My breath caught. It mattered very much. I'd stuff envelopes, deliver pizzas, clean bathrooms. I'd do honest work for honest pay.

At that moment I saw Mrs. Feldman walking toward me. I stood, knowing she was not about to sit on the step.

"You did the right thing."

"No, I rambled like a fool. I thought I was going to implode."

"Yes, but you spoke from the heart instead of your head. That's not always a bad thing. Sharing your fears and secrets is never easy. I think everyone in there knows that. I know I certainly do."

"Does that mean you've told your sons about Elizabeth?"

"I have."

"Can I ask what happened?"

"Of course you can, dear, but don't you want to talk about what happened in there?"

"No, not really."

"Well, there was some yelling, a little crying, a *lot* of talking."

"And you told them that Andrew is trying to find her?"

"I did. And I told them that's thanks to you. They're having a little trouble processing it all. The sister, the letter from Sol. Things would have been very different. For all of us."

I looked away and coughed instead of cried. "I don't know what I'd have done without you through all this."

She tugged and I turned back. "The movers come next Monday, dear. But you're not getting rid of me that easily."

"Izzy Lane!"

The words smacked the back of my head and I turned around to face Jade. Her shoes were off and her face was red.

"Geraldine, do you mind if I talk to Izzy alone?"

Mrs. Feldman sandwiched my hand between hers and pulled away. "No matter what happens, you'll be fine," she mouthed, and walked away.

"I'm sorry," I said to Jade. "I am so, so sorry."

"How could you lie to me? To *me*? I don't even know who you are. It's like you've been faking this friendship for twenty years."

"I have not!"

"You lied to me over and over again."

"I was embarrassed!"

"With me?"

"I was alone and that made me feel awful. And then Bruce lost his job and I was scared. . . . I'm going to pay you back."

"This isn't about the money! I'd have lent you money. Hell, I'd have given you money. You know that. Of all the people in the world, you didn't think *I'd* understand what it was like to be single when all your friends are married? How about the fact that all my friends have husbands *and* children and I don't want either? Don't you think I'm an outsider? That I feel different? No, because you didn't think. You didn't think enough of me to trust me. You're not who I thought you were. Not at all."

Our twenty-year friendship faltered and flashed before me like an old-fashioned slide show. Jade had taken my lies as affronts on our friendship, and on her worth as my friend, not just as assaults on my own character.

"It's no excuse, but I am *so* not where I thought I'd be when I turned forty," I said.

"Give me a break! Who is?"

"You. Rachel. My brothers. Bruce."

"You really think Bruce is where he thought he'd be? In a new job with less pay and living alone in the suburbs? I doubt it."

I shrugged.

"Oh, and are you going to leave out the fact that Rachel knew?"

"I tried to tell you!"

Jade rolled her eyes. "Not hard enough."

I had no defense.

"God, I thought we'd have more time together now. You ruined it. You ruined us."

"I can fix it. Let me fix this. Please!"

"For God's sake, Izzy, get over yourself. I have. And now I have to go salvage what's left of my career."

Jade walked away without hesitation, pushed around the revolving door, and kept going. I felt an ache, then a snap. Jade broke my heart.

But not before I'd broken hers.

Andrew hurried across the lobby, but when he saw me, he stopped.

I hadn't moved but was breathless. "Jade left."

"What did you expect?"

Though it felt like months, it only was a week. The final boxes were being carried out of Mrs. Feldman's house by the time I arrived home from work. I hadn't stayed late, hoping to bear witness, and, as always, hoping that Jade had called and left a message. Not only had I been reduced to an every-other-week mother—but one without a best friend, and now I'd be one without a next-door neighbor. While I felt demoted, Noah had been catapulted to the top of Bruce's priority list. Mrs. Feldman was off on a new adventure at eighty-five. My happiness for each of them outweighed my self-pity. For that I was grateful. But I needed a new identity. Maybe I would dig out some of Noah's costumes. Capes could be empowering.

I walked into the Feldman house without knocking or yelling. Ray was standing in the middle of the empty living room, pivoting from side to side, holding a bulging trash bag.

"Hi, Elizabeth," he said, mimicking his mother. "It looks big in here without furniture, doesn't it? Lots of potential for a buyer."

"It just looks sad and empty to me."

Ray shrugged, and my thoughts tumbled off his shoulders and into the bag with the rest of the garbage. "Moving on to new and better things, I say."

"New isn't always better."

"I don't think moving on is your area of expertise, now, is it?"

I grimaced. Just because I'd moved back to where I'd grown up didn't mean I wasn't moving forward. I had done a lot of new and different things since my divorce. I'd . . . well, it didn't matter what I'd done or hadn't done before.

"Ma says you're comfortable here."

"I am."

"I say comfortable is the kiss of death. That's why we wanted Ma out of here. Nothing personal, but she needs to meet new people and do new things in a new place or she's going to wither up. And I'd say she's got a good decade left. Y'know what I mean?"

Why did Ray sound as if he'd grown up a hoodlum instead of as the son of a bookkeeper in what was once a nice Jewish neighborhood? "Where is your *ma*, by the way? I wanted to return this." I wanted to see her. I needed to remind myself I wasn't completely alone. I held out the pirate box and the key.

Ray grabbed the duo without an apology. "She left hours ago. It's bingo night."

Two weeks later and I still couldn't fall asleep until midnight. Two hours to go. What was I going to do for two hours? Facebook? TV? Read a book? It was too late to call Rachel. How I missed the days of random texts and phone calls at odd hours with Jade, ones that filled the time faster than a gushing fire hydrant had filled Good Street on a hot summer day. The house was quiet, but I didn't want to play music because then I might miss an errant creepy noise, one I'd have to investigate on my own. I looked in the coat closet and peeked down into the basement. I opened and closed the fridge three times; the cabinets, four. I had no appetite. Even when Noah was home with me next week, and even when someone bought the house next door, things wouldn't be the same.

Maybe things weren't supposed to be the same.

The obvious popped to mind like the early-spring crocuses. I knew this city, and where the still-good neighborhoods and the schools were. I also knew Bruce was apartment hunting, and where. No reason we shouldn't live close enough for Noah's sake yet far enough apart for our own sakes. No reason Noah couldn't be in a new school for first grade. No reason my parents couldn't finally sell this house or rent it.

It didn't matter how fast I went . . . just that I kept going.

I jittered with anticipation—stopped myself for the hundredth time that day from texting Jade—grabbed my laptop, and tapped my fingers while the screen came to life, ready for me to find the perfect new home. Just then, Felix jumped from the floor to the kitchen windowsill. A perfect new home that allowed cats.

But as I typed my wish list for bedrooms and bathrooms into tiny Web-site boxes, I knew what else I wished.

I pulled out Andrew's business card from the silverware drawer. Andrew had run ads on *Philly over Forty* with the belief that I was sharing real-life stories with readers. He'd admired the way I wrote about Mac. Maybe my lies had impacted his business as well as his ego. Jade wouldn't talk to me, but maybe Andrew would. I wanted to apologize, wish him well, and then I wanted to move on.

Who was I kidding? I wanted to hear his voice.

The anxiety that anchored me to my cell phone was worse than when I'd sat by the Princess phone in the apartment Jade and I shared our senior year at Penn.

This new kind of angst was *mobile*—so for more than a week now, I'd been reminded that Andrew had not acknowledged my voice mail just as he hadn't acknowledged my e-mail, and I'd been reminded of that whether I was in the bathroom, at school, or in the supermarket.

How was *this* social progress?

Maybe I didn't deserve acknowledgment, but I did deserve closure. I wanted to apologize, if not face-to-face, at least voice-to-voice, but I hadn't been given that option. I stared at Andrew's business card for a hint or direction. It was time to forgive myself for being unforgivable. I tore the card in half and then looked at each piece.

The answer had been there all along.

After work the next day I drove into Center City and beat most of the traffic. But I wouldn't have cared if the drive had taken hours.

The building was tall and glass and stood like a soldier among its brothers. The lobby had a metal detector but I could get in without ID. I had the element of surprise on my side, although last time that didn't work so well.

The elevator doors opened on the twenty-third floor, and I, along with others, poured out. I turned right for Suite 2320. The door was plain and simple.

ANDREW MANN, ATTORNEY AT LAW

I turned the doorknob. Locked. Andrew wasn't working at four o'clock on a Monday? Of course not! He had two kids who still needed car seats, like Noah. Andrew could be anywhere. Soccer, dance, the dentist, the doctor, the car-pool line. He could be in court. With a client. On vacation.

I knocked and waited. I knocked again. I unclenched my fists when I realized I was digging my nails into my palms. I had lied, but I had also confessed. Publicly. And I apologized. Privately. The least Andrew could have done was acknowledge the effort. Say okay. Say thanks. Say go to hell. Say anything.

The door opened.

"Hey."

All of a sudden, I had nothing to say.

"I was in the neighborhood . . ."

"Okay . . ."

"Can I come in? I won't take much of your time."

"Okay."

The waiting room looked like a living room. One that'd had a woman's touch.

"Sorry I knocked so loud." There I go lying again.

"I lock the door if I don't have any appointments scheduled. Which I don't."

"Who is it, Daddy?"

A little girl with long brown hair slinked out of a back room. She was more tween than toddler.

"Paige, this is Ms. Lane. Would you give us a few minutes? You can play on the computer."

She smiled at me with a mouthful of braces before turning away.

"She's adorable," I said.

"Thanks."

"She looks too old for a booster, though."

Andrew cocked his head.

"I saw them in your car. The booster seats?"

"Oh, no. Paige is eleven. The boosters are for the twins. They're three and a half."

"Boys or girls?"

"One of each."

"Three kids. Wow."

"No, four kids. Zoe's eight."

"Wow."

"Yeah, it usually gets that reaction. Widower, dad, four kids. We also have a dog, a snake, a turtle, and many stuffed animals, along with a vast assortment of sports equipment and art supplies. The dot paints are my personal favorite, which really makes me a chick magnet."

"I'm sure it does." I nodded and my throat burned. Andrew was not just a good dad, he was a great dad. His ocean-deep loss did not drown his soccer sensibilities and playdate priorities. Or his sense of humor. If that didn't make a guy attractive, what did? Jade had known all along. I swallowed, and the heat traveled to my ears and then hijacked my body from the top down.

"Truly, Elizabeth? I was being sarcastic. Is there something in particular you wanted?"

"Sorry. I just wanted to say . . . I was thinking . . . I just wanted to say I was sorry. In person. I didn't know if you got my voice mail. Or my e-mails." Oh, how I had rambled in those e-mails.

"I did."

"Did you read the e-mails?"

"I did."

"Did you listen to the voice mail?"

"I did."

"You didn't answer them."

"No, I didn't."

I shrugged. Eloquence had left the building. "I guess I thought—I hoped—that we were friends. Or that maybe we were becoming friends. That maybe you could forgive me. I guess I was wrong. I won't bother you again."

I almost turned to leave through the open door, but Andrew put his hand on my shoulder. Even through my trench coat, the pressure rooted me. I wanted him to ask me to stay, to talk, to explain myself, to apologize again. "I liked you, Elizabeth, but how I felt doesn't matter. You lied to your best friend for months, not to mention to me and everyone else. I don't have the time or the energy for games."

"I lost my best friend and I humiliated myself in public. Believe me, I don't have the time or energy for games either. I've said I'm sorry a thousand times, and I've meant it every time. Now I'm done." I looked at him. We were eye to eye. I looked right in and through. Andrew wasn't as short as I'd thought.

"I believe you're sorry and I wish you the best. If we ever bump into each other, I hope it won't be awkward."

"Absolutely not." Another lie. I looked away.

"Good." Both his hands gripped the door handle, ready to close it behind me, shutting me out the way I deserved.

"How *is* Jade? She won't return my calls or e-mails either."

"She's fine. She's angry and hurt, but she's fine."

"I saw the new Web site. And the advice column. I'm glad it worked out."

Silence.

"Why did you let me in?"

"I'm not sure."

— Chapter 27 —

Olly Olly Oxen Free

THE LOBBY AT SHADY Forest Retirement Village smelled like bleach and scalloped apples. It wasn't a bad smell, just more institutional than residential. Until we walked into Mrs. Feldman's apartment. Then it just smelled like home.

In the two months since she'd moved to Shady Forest, I had stopped asking about her Elizabeth. She had stopped asking about Jade. I knew we both still thought of them all the time.

Mrs. Feldman's gaze shifted from me to her shelves, which were filled with photos and displayed the pirate box. "Let's take a walk. I want to show you something."

Noah pushed the elevator button and we rode down to the second floor. The community room was dotted with card tables. The library had books and CDs, DVDs, and computers. Mrs. Feldman opened the door and led us inside.

"I love having these computers right downstairs. Hi, Marv."

A man with his back to us raised his hand in a wave. "Hi, Deeny."

"Deeny?" I raised my eyebrows.

"Oh, never mind Marv. He's a big flirt."

We settled Noah at a table with a stack of children's books, intended for just such a purpose. Then Mrs. Feldman sat in front of a computer and pulled out the drawer with the keyboard. She typed with an ease that erased any notion of arthritis. Mrs. Feldman had made friends. Flirty friends. She was busy and happy. Ray had been right. About more than his mother.

I scooted a chair close. I half expected Mrs. Feldman to click on my new blog, cleverly titled *Izzy's Blog*. This was the one I started just for me, without fanfare or a fake name. I'd shown it to her in case she wanted to read it. She had. To date, Mrs. Feldman and Ethan were the only people to comment. That was okay. I was writing it just for me, as I should have been doing all along. I even showed it to Noah, although he didn't read it. No secrets or lies.

I'd learned my lesson. Deeply. I'd apologized. Sincerely. Now I'd transform my life. Purposefully. I'd do it without Mrs. Feldman next door, without contempt for Bruce, without Jade as my best friend. I wished some things were different, but I not only needed to move forward, I wanted to.

"I wish I'd gotten to know Andrew better," I said.

"Where did that come from?"

"Just thinking out loud."

"Maybe you should stop thinking so much. You'll find someone, Elizabeth. Or someone will find you. Probably where and when you least expect it."

I was tired of the when-you-least-expect-it and lid-for-every-pot clichés, but just nodded. Then an unfamiliar Web site appeared on the oversize monitor.

"Look. These are all women who gave up babies at the Lakeview Home. Some of us are looking for our children; some just want to know other girls who gave away babies. We share photos and stories. Some just want to talk about these difficult things with strangers." I could relate. "We started an online support group." Mrs. Feldman tapped her forefinger to her chest. "I'm the moderator. You see, Elizabeth? The Internet can be used *for good.*"

I didn't know who was writing Pop Philly's new advice column, but it didn't matter. I had to send an e-mail of my own. To a stranger. An e-mail to a stranger that might end up public.

Well, it wasn't like I had to save face.

From: Izzy Lane <izzylane@email.com>

To: Ask Anything <AskAnything@Pop_Philly.com>

Subject: Desperately Seeking Jade

Dear Ask Anything,

Your editor, Jade, was my best friend for more than twenty years. I don't know if you'll publish this letter, or even respond, but I do know that Jade is likely reading all or most of the letters that come in. She's hands-on that way, until she trusts you completely. The way she used to trust me.

And that's why I'm here.

I made a mistake when I allowed Jade and my cousin to believe something—someone—and none of it was true. Then I took it further, way off course, by perpetuating the lie online. Crazy, right? I know.

The thing is, sometimes we get lost in our own pity, and it's hard to see through the muck. That's when we do things we never thought we'd do, things we said we'd never do, things we've judged others for doing.

I have to admit that aside from the fact that my best friend has cut me off, I have gained a lot from this experience, through my grave error in judgment. I have realized that I often don't give the people closest to me enough credit. Had someone come to me with the same story—anywhere along the way—I'd have tried to understand. Why didn't I know that others would do the same, especially Jade? I have also learned that it's much harder to lie and keep secrets than it is to tell the truth. Even when the truth causes big, ugly problems.

With those lessons learned, and apologies made, I just don't know what else to do to prove to Jade that this will never happen again. If she doesn't talk to me, how will she know? At least I can move forward knowing I've apologized again. Please tell Jade I keep buying Goldfish crackers, which I don't like, and my son eats too many of, because I'm hoping that she will show up at my door. For the record, when she's angry or upset, she eats them by the handfuls.

I'm reading Pop Philly every day, and as always, I am very proud of Jade. Maybe I don't have the right to be proud anymore. Pride connotes some kind of propriety; it's felt by someone who's emotionally invested. I guess I always will be.

Thanks for your time.

Sincerely,

Izzy Lane

My weeks without Noah started to pass more quickly, until the day he was coming home. Now Bruce would be dropping off Noah in half an hour, so it was crunch time. Literally. I had never been a fitness freak, but I figured forty was the time to start introducing my body to exercise. Plus, I was moving to a walk-up in a walkable neighborhood. I didn't want the neighbors to think I was unfit in any way. I lay on my back on the floor, knees up, hands behind my head. One, two, three, four. Take a break. Five. Five sit-ups. Five was a good number to start with, I was sure of it.

The doorbell rang. I'd missed hearing Bruce pull up and didn't care that he was early. Noah was home with me for the next week.

"Coming!" I yelled to the front door, but always forgot to ask if the person on the other side had heard me.

"Welcome home!" I said as I pulled open the door. It wasn't Noah. "Jade?"

"Is this a bad time?"

"No, no. Come in. I was just exercising."

"That's new."

And so much more.

I stepped aside and Jade walked in. Her steps were tentative, but they were steps nonetheless.

"I read the letter you sent to *Ask Anything*. I read most of them."

"I figured."

"But that's not why I'm here."

"It's not?"

"No, I'm here because of Drew. *Andrew.*"

I gulped. I'd tried so hard to place him to the side of my thoughts, back behind the lessons learned, opportunities missed, and packed boxes. Now was she coming to tell me that I'd been right all along? That they were together? "What did he say?"

"That I needed to think long and hard about what happened to decide if it was really worth ending our friendship over."

I couldn't speak.

"And my answer was no."

No, she didn't want to be friends—or no, she didn't want to end the friendship? My mind jumbled with anticipation, fear, delight, and worry. Jade looked at me and shook her head, releasing me from my trance.

"Earth to Pea—you mentioned something about *Goldfish*?"

I ran to the pantry. "Yes! I have pizza, cheddar, and Parmesan, and even those new chocolatey ones."

"I'll take my old favorite."

I tore open a bag of pizza Goldfish and handed it to her. "So—we're okay?"

Jade tipped back her head, then stopped before lifting the bag to her lips. "Not yet," she said. "But we will be."

It was mid-July, the first time the temperature had poked above ninety with humidity to match. It was also moving day. Noah, with a snorkel mask perched on his head, walked with me through each empty room one more time. We pointed to each corner and counted one, two, three, four, as if we could inadvertently have packed one into a box. I memorized the outlines on the carpets and the walls made by furniture and photographs. I'd snapped pictures with my phone before the movers arrived, most photobombed by Noah, which would one day seem the perfect memento of our year. At the end of August, Matthew would move in for his internship at Jeanes Hospital. My nephew, the doctor, would continue the Lane tradition on Good Street, at least for a year or so.

My new neighborhood beckoned louder than a smoke alarm. The Art Museum, Boathouse Row, the Barnes Foundation, and Kelly Drive, not to mention the Oval and Fairmount Park. Bruce had moved into his loft in May. My apartment was four blocks away on a tree-lined side street, a half block from Noah's new elementary school. He already knew the fastest route between Dad's house and Mom's—in a car, on a bike, and by foot. A horn sounded and Noah's eyes grew wide. His expectations held no melancholy. How glad I was for that.

"Time to go," I said.

We walked downstairs, and I held open the screen door all the way and blew a kiss to Maya and Ethan. Noah hustled into the backseat with his cousin.

"Are you sure you don't want us to stay?" Ethan yelled.

"I'm sure." I needed to do this alone.

One last time, I walked into my parents'—my—bedroom. Something onion-tasting—chive cream cheese maybe, from the night before, stopped at the base of my throat and then went back where it belonged.

The windows were still open, the air was off. I leaned against the wall and looked out and up at the sky, cut in half by the telephone wire that had carried my teenage chatter. Then I looked down and watched Marina, the little girl who'd moved into the Feldman house—the Ramirez house—playing hopscotch in a pink bathing suit and then skipping up to our steps until she was out of sight.

I was glad a little girl was in that house now. Again. Still.

I walked through the other bedrooms again, gazed out the windows, then went back to mine. I leaned in and searched the empty clothes closet. I heard a *tap-tap-tap* on the wall and turned around.

Andrew wore khaki shorts, leather flip-flops, and a vintage-looking Coca-Cola T-shirt. He held a blue container of salt and a loaf of bread. According to Jewish tradition, these were the first items I should bring into my new home. They signified that I'd sustain myself there. I hoped that tradition was on point.

"The door was open," he said.

My throat constricted and then relaxed. "It's been a long time." More than three months, had I been counting.

"You're not an easy woman to find."

"Excuse me?"

"I thought you already moved, so I went by your new place and no one was there. Then I drove here, and up the street a few times, but didn't see your car."

"It's in the driveway. How did you know . . . ?" Any of it?

"Jade." We said it at the same time.

Andrew looked around the room. "Where's your little pirate buddy?"

"He's a snorkeler now. My brother took him and my niece to lunch."

"I won't keep you. I just wanted to bring you these."

"I thought you were angry with me."

"I *was* angry with you." He swung the loaf of bread from side to side. "But I couldn't stop thinking about you. Jade said I needed to take my own advice and decide if what happened was really worth never seeing you again."

A gazillion points for Jade.

Andrew walked to the middle of the empty room, footsteps light, but shoes flapping against his heels. He set the bread and the salt on the floor. I walked to him and Andrew slid his fingers through mine with ease.

He squeezed my hand. Or I squeezed his. I wasn't sure. Did it matter? And did all hands fit together this well?

"I thought I'd never see you again, let alone be friends."

"I don't want to be friends."

I pulled my hands to my sides and stepped back.

Andrew took one baby step toward me. "I want to be *more* than friends."

My heart was pounding so loud I wasn't sure I'd heard him, but it was time to trust my instincts. No more playing, pretending, or hiding. I had to be open and honest—with Andrew and with myself.

"Me, too."

He smiled, sweet and broad, but then his mouth turned down, his expression pensive. Was he changing his mind? That fast?

"I have to warn you." He shook his head. I gulped, still transfixed, as my arms went cold, almost numb. "I kill at Chutes and Ladders. Not to mention Angry Birds."

Noah *loved* that game. The feeling returned to my limbs, with little prickles of hope. "I'll just take you down during Pretty Pretty Princess."

"Oh, you haven't seen anything till you've seen me in a tiara."

I couldn't wait.

Alone on Good Street for the last time, I sat on my top step, legs out in front of me. The hot, rough cement scratched against my little-girl, teenager, grown-up bare calves. I rubbed my thumbs along the familiar bumps. A new neighbor, one I'd never know, waved from across the street and I waved back. Marina splashed in her wading pool, her mother reading a magazine. A bus screeched to a halt at the corner. Horns beeped. Air-conditioner window units cranked, hummed, and dripped a steady beat. A potato-chip bag skittered down the sidewalk on a humid breeze, too fast for me to catch it. It was time to go but I stuck to the step as if I'd sat on a giant wad of bubble gum. Will Noah like his new school? Will my neighbors like me? Did I empty the fridge? Remember the keys? With one hand I grabbed the metal railing that had so often prevented my falls. I squeezed until it burned my palm and soothed my nerves.

Then my childhood burst into my head and hugged my heart. Water from the hose. A Texas Tommy at the diner. Late summer nights on the steps. Unlocked front doors. Mom's doctored matzo-ball soup from a jar. The smells filled my nose. The tastes coated my mouth.

All the memories tethered me.

And then they said, *Let's go.*

Acknowledgments

The story in this book, as well as my own story, would be very different if my parents hadn't moved to our Northeast Philadelphia neighborhood in 1969. Mom and Dad, I can't imagine a better place for David and me to have grown up. Thank you.

I am incredibly fortunate to have friends in Philadelphia whom I've held dear since before instant-access communication, when long-distance calls cost extra, and letters written by hand took days to arrive. These friends have rallied around, answered many questions, and appeased every writer—and every other—whim while I wrote *The Good Neighbor*: Joanne Beaver, Larry Blumenthal, Tom Brett, John Caruso, Steven Citron, Jodi Cohen Levine, Carole Farley, Diane Pascali, Sheree Richman, Mindy Saifer Cohen, Eric Schlanger, Scott Segal, and my sister-friend, Judith Soslowsky. Blakely Minton from Redfin shared her expert knowledge of current Philadelphia neighborhoods and real estate trends with graciousness and good humor.

This book would not exist without Christina Gombar, who

urged me to watch the 1945 film *Christmas in Connecticut*, which introduced me to the original Elizabeth Lane character, gently inspiring my own. Heartfelt thanks to Therese Walsh for challenging me to write outside my comfort zone. Alice Davis, Tina Ann Forkner, Fern Katz, Annmarie Lockhart, and Renee San Giacomo for reading and loving Izzy like I do. Renee Rosen for collaborating over four-hour "working" lunches. Lori Nelson Spielman, Pamela Toler, and Julie Kibler for friendships that go far beyond writing. Manny Katz, I'm sorry your title, or photo, didn't make it onto this book cover. I still owe you one.

To my Book Pregnant tribe, the Women's Fiction Writers Association, and Tall Poppy Writers—your support is beyond compare.

To the wonderful and loyal readers of my Women's Fiction Writers blog, rest assured, every word there is true.

I'm so lucky to have had Brenda Copeland, Laura Chasen, and the whole St. Martin's Press team championing me (and Izzy) through every phase of this book. Jason Yarn believed in Izzy's story from the first time I mentioned it. Danielle Egan-Miller, Joanna MacKenzie, Abby Saul, and Molly Foltyn adopted Izzy (and me) as their own. Ladies, I look forward to many years of crying over tacos with you.

To the readers, book club members, booksellers, and librarians, notably Megan Millen of the Flossmoor Library, who asked for book two with enthusiasm. I am thrilled to finally share *The Good Neighbor*.

And, of course, to Zachary and Chloe, I love you, and hope the message is clear. No matter where it happens to be, I'm always home.

Discussio
Question

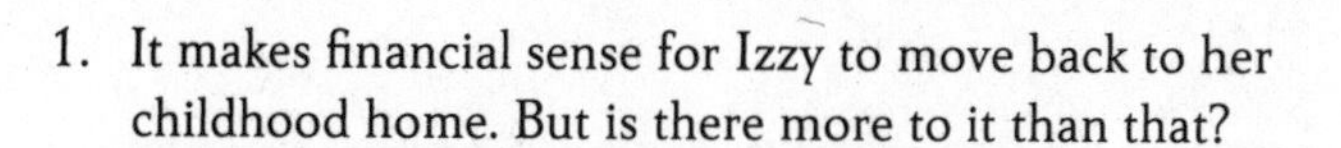

1. It makes financial sense for Izzy to move back to her childhood home. But is there more to it than that?

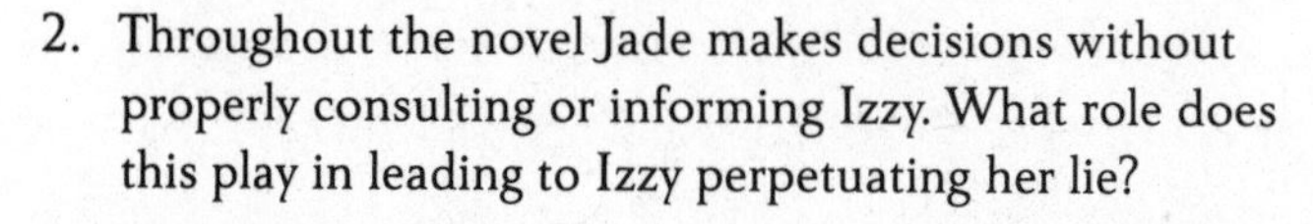

2. Throughout the novel Jade makes decisions without properly consulting or informing Izzy. What role does this play in leading to Izzy perpetuating her lie?
3. Does Bruce have a right to demand equal custody of Noah? Would it be better for Noah to share equal time with Bruce and Izzy or to continue spending most of his time with Izzy?
4. As Izzy contemplates Bruce's influence on Noah, she recalls how her own brothers strived to emulate their father growing up, and the pride this brought to their father. How important is a male role model in the life of a young child? In the absence of Bruce, could Ethan or Andrew play the role of surrogate father to Noah?
5. What effect does a new partner like Amber play on the development of a young child? How do you think Noah will feel about Andrew coming into his life?
6. By the end of the book, Mrs. Feldman, despite her initial misgivings, seems happy in her assisted-living environment. Is it simply the change of scenery or does it have more to do with coming clean of her own secret?
7. Izzy, Bruce, and Mrs. Feldman all have new living arrangements by the end of the book. How important is a new house to a new start? Can a home have too much emotional baggage?
8. Despite Izzy's warnings, Rachel ends up taking things a bit too far with her old flame Jeremy. To what extent is catching up with an old ex acceptable?
9. Has your best friend ever kept an important secret from you? Can a friendship properly mend after a major betrayal?
10. Who is the good neighbor? Is it Mrs. Feldman or Izzy?